I SPIED ... SE

MARK ... N

Other Titles by Mark Timlin

MARK TIMLIN

I SPIED A PALE HORSE

First published in Great Britain by Toxic 1999

This edition published in 1999 by Toxic, an imprint of CT Publishing, PO Box 5880, Edgbaston, Birmingham, B16 8JF

A CIP catalogue record for this book is available from the British Library.

ISBN 1902002-17-2

9 8 7 6 5 4 3 2 1

Typography & Cover Design by DP Fact and Fiction

Printed and bound in Great Britain.

For Walden Robert Cassotto
1936—1973

I spied a pale horse
and a pale rider upon it
The name of the horse was pestilence
And the name of the rider was death

It's the end of the world as we know it
And I feel fine

—REM

IT WAS VERY QUIET in the meadow where we were lying. Just the sound of the warm breeze from the west playing through the long grass, a cricket chirping somewhere close, and in the trees to our left, two birds having a territorial argument. It was almost uncanny the way it was now, with no sounds of planes coming down in a landing pattern towards Heathrow or Gatwick, no helicopters following the motorway towards London, no cars, no music or the ambient sound of millions of people trying to live their lives in too close proximity to one another. I doubted now if there were millions of people on the entire planet.

I lay on my back and looked up at the blue bowl that used to be the Suffolk sky, and now was whatever you liked to call it, because counties and countries and territorial borders meant nothing, and watched a pair of butterflies flit from flower to flower. There were more butterflies that summer I swear. Or maybe I'd never taken time to notice them before.

Even Puppy was quiet. She knew the rules. She lay in the grass beside me, her body stretched full out, her tail just twitching occasionally, her head on her paws with an inch of her pink tongue jutting out of her mouth, and her eyes on me all the time. She was the only female I had any relationship with these days and that was the way I liked it.

I reached down with my right hand and placed it on the velvet skin that covered her skull between her ears and she moved her head round so she could lick my wrist.

I looked over towards Ugly. He lay half in and half out of a dry ditch on the other side of the rough track that ran through the meadow. He nodded to me and I nodded back. He was massive, built like the proverbial brick shithouse, and the strongest man I'd ever met. Not for the first time I was glad he was on my side. Once upon a time he must have had a proper name but I didn't know it. Ugly was what he wanted to be called and that was OK by me. He was bloody ugly, that was a fact, but he put it about something shocking.

And then I heard it. The sound we'd been waiting for: the sound of horse's hooves, the creak of harness and the rumble of wooden wheels. I looked over at Ugly again and he nodded for a second time and there was a wolfish grin on his face.

I held the barrel of the pump action shotgun I was carrying in my left hand and waited for the horse and cart to come closer.

I knew exactly what ordnance we were carrying. That was my job. I had a five shot Winchester pump fully loaded with twelve gauge shells, plus another five spare. Under my right arm was a US Army Colt .45 of indeterminable age with a full seven shot magazine and one spare clip. Under my left was one of my faithful Glock 17's with a full magazine. The other was in a holster strapped around my waist. Both were fully loaded, but I had no spare ammunition. It was a constant worry. In my boot was a six shot .38 Colt Commando and another twenty shells for it in the pocket of my leather jacket. Ugly had a twelve gauge up and under shotgun with a sawn off barrel and stock. In a bag slung round his neck he carried ten spare cartridges. In his pocket was a Webley .455 revolver loaded with six bullets and a half box of loose shells. That was our entire arsenal. But it was enough. For now.

In the late nineties when new handgun laws had come into force I knew that almost twenty-six million rounds of ammunition had been destroyed. I wish we had some of those now. Of all the shortages since the Death, ammunition for our weapons was the worst. In my dreams I found a stash of full metal jackets hidden somewhere in England. Thousands and thousands of brass cartridges that made my mouth water. And even when I was awake I dreamed of the same thing… Maybe one day.

As the cart drew closer so that I could almost smell the horse's sweat I came suddenly to my feet and saw a lone young man driving the rig. He was no more than twenty with long blonde hair and he wore a denim jacket over raggedy blue jeans.

Ugly rose beside me and we pointed our carry weapons at the boy. 'Stand and deliver,' I said. 'Your money or your life.' Just like Dick Turpin in days of old. That's what we are. Highwaymen. It's a growth industry.

'Oh shit,' said the boy as he pulled hard on the reins and reached under his jacket with his right hand.

Ugly shot him in the head, the balls of lead blowing half his skull off his shoulders and he slumped back in the seat of the wagon.

The horse reared at the sound and Ugly reached over, grabbed the bridle and held tightly until it calmed down, speaking softly to the animal all the time. I knew he'd been something of a country boy but he didn't like to talk about it. Didn't like to talk about much. But that was his business. Everyone who'd survived The Death had horror stories. I had my own and I didn't talk about them either.

'I hope that was a gun he was reaching for,' I said when the echoes of the shot had died away and Dobbin stopped pawing the ground. 'Or you've wasted a cartridge.'

'Too bad if it wasn't,' said Ugly. Like I said, I was glad he was on my side.

I walked towards the cart, which was fully loaded at the back, just as we'd hoped, and climbed up next to the driver. He didn't look in too great shape but I was used to dead bodies and I felt under his jacket and came up with a shitty old Sterling .32 automatic in a shoulder holster. Damn. I'd been hoping for a 9mm. I checked the clip in the gun's butt. Six shells. I tossed the pistol to Ugly. 'Yours, I believe,' I said.

Ugly smiled a rare smile and dropped the gun into his bag. I searched the driver but he had no more bullets, just a pack of cigarettes and a lighter, which I kept for myself. Ugly didn't smoke. None of us would for much longer, but a cigarette is a cigarette is a cigarette.

I jumped down and went to check the load. Puppy joined me. 'Shit,' I said. 'There's brains and all sorts all over this.' I found a rag under the driver's seat and mopped up as best I could. Puppy was licking at some blood on the road and I pushed her away with my boot. 'Don't do that Puppy,' I said. 'It's not nice.'

She stopped. She knew to obey me. That was the rule. My way or on your way.

The flatbed of the cart was stacked with goodies. Crates of wine and beer and scotch. A huge can of petrol which was almost as scarce as ammunition, plastic wrapped cartons of canned food, including enough dog food to keep Puppy happy for a year, unless we humans had to start eating it first, clothes, boots, tools and pots and pans. There was even four hundred Benson & Hedges king sized that brought a smile to my face. They were more precious than gold these days. What I didn't smoke I'd barter. It was a real tinker's wagon. Obviously the boy had been an entrepreneur, venturing into the stench and danger of some town and liberating enough goods to sell from tiny settlement to tiny settlement. It was a shame we'd had to close him down. But that was the breaks.

'You want to go get the truck,' I said to Ugly. 'We'd better split before someone comes along.'

He vanished into the undergrowth and I heard the grind of a starter motor and he forced the Land Rover we were driving through a hedge and on to the track and drove it up tight to the cart.

We siphoned some of the petrol straight into the tank and as always I hoped it hadn't been contaminated which would mean a breakdown and I'd watch as Ugly cleared the fuel lines. We got to work and within minutes we'd transferred the gear from the cart into the back of the truck.

Ugly unharnessed the horse and it wandered further into the meadow and started grazing at the grass. We left the boy where he was and reversed the Land Rover back to the tarmac road and headed Northeast.

After twenty miles or so as the sun started to sink towards the horizon we made camp and Ugly set about preparing some food. I opened a can of the newly liberated dog food and fed Puppy, who after she'd eaten immediately settled down and went to sleep.

After we'd eaten, Ugly and I spread out sleeping bags by the fire and I lit one of the boy's cigarettes.

'Those things'll kill you,' said Ugly.

'That'll be a relief,' I said, and lay back and let my mind wander to different times when everything seemed so settled and my worst fear was lung cancer.

2

AS FAR AS I CAN WORK IT OUT, and work it out I've tried a million times, it all started when someone exploded a nuclear bomb in the old USSR. To this day no one really knows who, and for sure now, no one ever will. It could've been some crazy old guard Cossack who was fed up with Russia becoming a third world country on a diet of Coca Cola, McDonalds hamburgers and satellite TV. Or maybe it was Saddam Hussein who figured that Boris Yeltsin wasn't giving him the backing he so desperately needed. Or maybe it was just a bomb that blew up by itself. There were a lot of warheads rotting away in Russia in those days. And for certain there still are. Maybe they're popping off now, one by one like a string of firecrackers. We'd never know. That is, we'd never know until our skin started peeling off our faces and all sorts of nasty cancerous growths started appearing on our extremities. That would be funny.

The Death wasn't far behind. And before communications broke down altogether there was a theory that somewhere close to ground zero there was a bacterial weapons dump and a lot of nasty germs were blown up into the stratosphere to drop like the gentle rain from heaven. The quality of mercy is not strained you see.

Or it might just have been that the planet grew tired of us, and shucked most of the human race off like bad skin. Weird things had been happening for years. Global warming, the melting of the ice at the poles, holes in the ozone layer, freak weather conditions. And that was just nature. We humans had been busy having our own *fin-de-siècle* as well. Violence, murder, strange religions, mass suicides, alien sightings, the works. Now I've never been of a green persuasion, but it seemed to me we'd lost touch with our environment. If you treated the planet Earth like a stranger, a piece of rock spinning through space and nothing more, then we were bound to come a cropper. And we had. All we were interested in was getting more money and a better house and a bigger car. But the earth was alive. I could feel it that night as I lay in my sleeping bag with

11

Puppy's head on my chest and Ugly lying on the other side of our camp. I felt it more and more every day. If we'd just given it the respect it deserved maybe we wouldn't have found ourselves in our present position, like the dinosaurs, heading for extinction. And we were. I could feel that too, so it matters little what people like Ugly and me do.

So it's all still a mystery where The Death came from. Ah, but isn't ignorance still bliss? And of course now it's of academic interest only. But at the time the bomb went off. Well, the whole world held its breath for a couple of days in case this was the big one. The one that everyone had been waiting for since the end of World War Two. Armageddon. The end of the world. But the media assured us it was a one-off. A dreadful accident. No problem. Get back to doing the *Sun* bingo and don't worry your pretty little heads, the four horsemen were still in the stable. And like fools we believed them, breathed again, and went back to getting ready for the biggest party in history, The Millennium. The year 2000.

But you see I was interested and I dug a little deeper. And I had an inside track because I was a policeman in those days. Yes. Strange as it may seem by the way I earn a crust these days, I was one of the thin blue line that kept society out of the hands of the vandals. And I wasn't a bad copper. I've seen and known worse. And I was married to the most beautiful woman in the world. Dominique was her name. Her grandmother had been French and she was named after her. She looked like a black-haired angel and acted like one too, and since the day we'd met I'd never really looked at another woman. We'd met when I'd been a beat copper and she'd been studying to become a medical researcher. I'd never thought I'd had a chance with her, but I persevered and succeeded in winning her heart. Then we had our baby. A little girl named Louisa, which was also from the French. I never cheated on my family, which was unusual for a man in my position. Because when you're a detective inspector in the Metropolitan Police, believe me there are many ways to cheat. Sexually, financially, as many as you can name. But I couldn't be bothered. I had the best at home, why settle for less somewhere else? Not that I didn't go to the odd CID dinner where strippers and lap dancers came out with the brandy and cigars. And sometimes there was lipstick on my collar when I left, but I'd make sure I had a clean shirt in the car and drop the dirty one off at a dry cleaners the next day. On the badness scale of one to ten I didn't reckon that was too awful. Not that it matters now. Not that anything matters now.

Some years before I was transferred to Scotland Yard I'd done a stint with the diplomatic protection squad and I still had a good friend at the Foreign Office. So after all the fuss about the bomb had died down I invited him out for a drink, which turned into dinner and asked him what had really happened.

We met in a dingy little pub off Whitehall. One of the few in the area that hadn't turned into a tourist trap.

It was hot night on the cusp of August and September and I had come straight from the Yard and was wearing a light summer suit. My contact, a senior undersecretary named Clive Price was sweating in a winter weight pinstripe three-piece when he arrived. I had a pint waiting. 'You're an angel John,' he said as he sank the first inch.

'I've been called many things…'

'Believe me. It's even hotter in the halls of power than it is in here.'

'I can imagine.'

'So what's the interest John?' he asked after he'd lit a cigarette I offered.

'Everyone's interested.'

'Maybe. We've tried to keep the media at bay as much as possible. Didn't want to start a panic.'

'I wonder if this country could panic anymore. We seem to have got more lethargic every year.'

'We thought it was a possibility. We seem now to have a central brain. Located somewhere near the anus. Remember the outpouring of grief over Diana?'

'Of course.'

'You were at the funeral weren't you?'

'I was protecting a foreign dignitary.'

'What from? Elton John's singing? Look I don't want to talk too much in here. Walls have ears. How about dinner? My club's just round the corner.'

I can hardly imagine the existence of gentlemen's clubs now.

'Sounds good,' I said. 'Nursery stodge. Perfect for the weather.'

'Don't you believe it John,' he said. 'We've got a new chef. He's a marvel. I promise he'll whip up something cool and light for us.'

We set off though the boiling streets on the short walk to Clive's club. It was in a massive, grey stone building on the other side of the Mall. Its walls streaked with layers of soot that looked like they'd stood for centuries and would stand for centuries more with no more than a nod to contemporary mores.

'Go on through to the bar,' said Clive when we passed through the massive wooden doors into the reception area. 'I'll sign you in and book a table. A swift one first though. Champagne I think. My usual. Just tell the barman to put it on my bill.'

I did as he said. It was blessedly cool inside the building and I could hear the faint throb of an air conditioning unit beneath my feet. Whatever the club looked like on the outside, inside it was obviously more than ready for the approaching new millennia.

Clive did the necessary with the porter on the desk and followed me through to the bar where the waiter had taken my order. 'Good,' said Clive. 'Might as well fiddle whilst Rome burns.' I felt a chill at his words that had nothing to do with the air conditioning.

We sat at a table and the barman brought over a bottle of Krug and two champagne flutes. He poured, Clive tasted, declared himself satisfied and the barman backed off gracefully.

'Did you mean that?' I asked when we were alone.

'What?'

'The crack about Rome burning.'

'We live in interesting times John,' he said. 'And remember that old Chinese curse?'

'May you live in interesting times,' I said.

'Precisely.'

'So what about this bomb? There's all sorts of stories going round.'

'We don't know,' he said holding out his arms wide, the hand that wasn't holding his glass palm outwards in the oldest way in the world to say 'I'm telling the truth.'

'Why not?'

'Because an area of five square miles just outside Odessa was decimated. Razed to the ground. And bang in the middle was the local radar and Air Traffic Control. We don't know if the bomb was incoming or detonated on the ground.'

'Was it all on its own?'

'Sorry?'

'Was it in a silo or a warehouse or slung under an aircraft? What?'

'We don't know John. All we do know is that at the epicentre of the blast there was a military airfield.'

'What about all those satellites that I've paid for with my tax money over the last ten years? I thought they could pick up a pin dropping in a darkened room.'

He looked embarrassed. 'You know how it is John. Some days nothing goes right. The satellite that keeps an eye on that particular piece of real estate was having problems that day.'

'How about the Yanks? Don't tell me their satellites were having problems too.'

'The *entente cordiale* is not all it could be at the moment. We're having some local difficulties with our friends in the west. They're playing it close to their chests and keeping all sorts of secrets.'

'How many people died?'

'Once again no real information. The Russkies…' he smiled at the word, '…are being a bit close mouthed. Christ, who can blame them? Imagine if that had happened in Missouri or Montana. Close to the chest wouldn't be in it…'

'Or the South Downs,' I interrupted.

'Don't.'

We finished the bottle of champagne and went into the restaurant where Clive had been right, the food had improved and we enjoyed a light supper gazing at the passers-by with their guidebooks and their backpacks.

'So everything's going to be just fine,' I said to Clive over the pudding course.

'Who knows?' he replied. 'We live in hope.'

But I still remembered what he'd said about Rome burning, and I was reminded when I spoke to him for the last time in early February the next year. He phoned me at home. 'John,' he said. 'Strange things are happening.'

'Like what?' I said.

'People are dying in Africa.'

'So what's new?' I asked. 'People are always dying in Africa.'

'This is different. Maybe you should take Dominique and Louisa out of town for a while.'

'Are you drunk Clive?' I asked.

'Permanently. Just do as I say. Happy New Year by the way. It may be our last.' And he hung up on me. I never spoke to him or saw him again. Sometimes I wonder if he's safe in some bunker somewhere with a bunch of politicos breathing recycled air and waiting for it to be safe enough to come out and form a government. I hope I'm around to see them and use up the last of our ammunition. But more likely he's dead too, like nearly everyone else.

That sticky night last summer after we'd drunk our coffee and brandy I went home by cab to the little house I shared with Dominique and Louisa in Clapham. Things were still so normal then, but somehow I could feel a change coming, like the way you can hear a train if you put your ear to the rails even though it's miles away, and I could do nothing about it.

And I'd been right. The change was to come frighteningly quickly and there were only mere months of the old way left before The Death came and nothing would ever be the same again.

I threw my cigarette into the fire and looked up at the sky. It was so black up there. A black that no one who had lived through the days of electricity had ever seen until The Death came. For the past fifty years or so the sky in this part of the hemisphere had reflected the lights of civilisation and had always had a slight orange glow. But now with electricity gone it was the texture of black velvet only lit by the moon and the stars, which on that night were almost bright enough to read by. And the satellites that I'd talked to Clive Price about were still up there, clearly visible as they sat above us and I wondered if they were still beaming photographs back down to earth. Photographs that no one would ever see, and I could feel the tears running down my cheeks at the thought of my wife and child, dead all those months since The Death was at its height. I only cry in the dark now so that no one can see. Tears for them, and all the others that have died, and for the way I am now killing the survivors as if there were people to spare.

THE MONTHS AFTER I saw Clive Price went by quickly. It was the autumn and early winter of 1999 and everyone was getting ready for the biggest celebration since time began. That old song by Prince was number one for sixteen weeks and you heard it everywhere you went. A friend of mine owned a penthouse on the Isle of Dogs with a huge terrace overlooking the Millennium Dome that was finally finished that October, and had guaranteed the party to end all parties on New Year's Eve. Dominique and I took Louisa with us. She wanted to stay up and see the million pound firework display that the government had been promising us for months. Louisa was seven years old then, still young enough to believe in Santa Claus, but old enough to participate in the more adult parts of the festivities like going to midnight mass on Christmas Eve and realising what it meant. Dominique and I had spent a fortune on presents and once she was fast asleep after church we piled brightly wrapped parcels around the tree in our living room. That Christmas was one of the best I could ever remember. I was glad that Louisa had died still believing in Santa Claus. It was a small mercy.

The New Year's Eve party was everything that my friend had promised and so were the fireworks. Louisa watched them yawning, but with a look of such joy on her face that I almost wept. Then Dominique and I put her down in our host's bedroom and danced until dawn.

It's one of the best memories that I carry with me now.

But the New Year brought all sorts of strange tidings.

First there was the Millennium bug that had caused such scares for the eighteen months or so before the clock struck twelve on that magical night. According to the media, all sorts of computers were going to crash as the twentieth century became the twenty-first and there'd be no electricity, no gas, no money from the banks, traffic lights wouldn't work and even your CD player would go into free fall and you wouldn't be able to listen to Prince anymore.

Which believe me would've been a blessing.

But in fact most things carried on as normal. Except that almost every burglar alarm in London seemed to go off as the laser beam shot from Greenwich Observatory across the river to the dome where the Queen and the Prime Minister were getting stuck into the *gratis* champagne and added a high pitched cacophony to the church bells and car horns and cheers and explosions that welcomed New Year's Day Two Thousand.

But a number of survivalists did take the warnings to heart and stockpiled food and bottled water and batteries and anything else they could think of during that time. Ugly and I have been grateful to them often as we've come across the remains of these caches on our travels.

You see it's an ill wind.

And after Clive Price phoned me with his doom-laden message I started to scan the newspapers every day.

What he'd said was true. People were dying in Africa. And Asia. And no one knew why. And people seemed to care less. There was a strange hangover in the country after the millennium celebrations. There'd been so much talk of new beginnings that the year Two Thousand was an anti climax.

But not for long.

I saw my first victim of The Death in a pub in Marylebone in late February. I'd been giving evidence in a manslaughter case at Marylebone Magistrate's Court that day and went for a pint with the prosecuting barrister when the court was adjourned. It was freezing cold outside, and we were knees in against the open fire in the corner when I noticed a young woman come in with two female friends and go to the bar. She was young and blonde and attractive in a long blue coat. She seemed to have a heavy cold and pulled a handkerchief from the pocket of her coat and blew her nose. But then February is cold and flu season in London.

Then, all of a sudden she went white and sweat broke out on her face like the tide coming in. She held onto the bar with one hand and tried to speak to the friend on her right who was ordering a round of drinks. But all that came out of her mouth was a gout of blood so red that I thought she was vomiting tomato soup and she fell forward, her face smacking against the polished surface of the bar before she crumpled to the floor in a heap.

Both her friends jumped and screamed and I stood up and ran towards them. 'I'm a policeman,' I said. 'Give her some air.' Then to the barman. 'Call an ambulance quickly.'

He stood transfixed and I shouted. 'Call nine-nine-nine NOW.'

He broke out of his trance and reached for the phone as I knelt beside the girl who couldn't have been more than twenty and I felt for her pulse. There was nothing, just the blood still oozing from her mouth and a long string of mucus coming from her nose.

I gave her heart massage and tried to force an air passage but her throat was constricted, and even though I gave her mouth to mouth it was no good.

Later I wondered if mouth to mouth had been such a good idea. But I'm immune to The Death you see. I worked it out roughly that point nought one of the human race are. If I hadn't been, I doubt I'd've lived for the rest of the week.

I was lucky. Or maybe unlucky. I leave you to work that one out for yourself.

The ambulance came about ten minutes later but she was dead. The paramedics took her away and I went back to my drink but couldn't touch it. She wasn't to be the last victim of The Death I was to see by a long way. But I'll always remember her. Someone told me her name was Susan. I never did find out her other name.

4

FROM THEN ON things moved fast. Too fast. Susan no-last-name was the first victim of The Death that I saw and touched. But she was by no means the last.

The next was a few days later in Queen Victoria Street as I was going to pick up a coffee from my favourite cafe on my way to work. At first I thought he was a drunk. A well dressed, smart looking drunk, but a drunk nevertheless. And starting rather early in the day. He was walking towards me in the direction of Victoria Station, weaving through the crowd knocking pedestrians out of his way. He was wearing a navy blue overcoat over a dark suit, white shirt and a maroon tie knotted neatly at his neck. He was carrying a black briefcase, which he dropped, and it burst spilling papers into the gutter. I saw him try to grab a woman's arm who pulled away alarmed and opened her mouth to remonstrate with him. But he ignored her words, tugged at his shirt collar, slumped against the front window of a shop so that the safety glass bowed, then fell to the pavement and lay perfectly still.

This time I didn't have to intervene as a passing squad car pulled up at the kerb immediately, and two uniformed officers emerged and went to his aid. One knelt over him then shook his head at his colleague who used his personal radio. A crowd had gathered and I watched for second before continuing on my way. It was just a small incident, the like of which happen a hundred, maybe a thousand times a day in the Metropolis.

There was only one strange thing. One thing that made it different. One thing that stuck in my mind. Both uniformed officers were wearing face masks. That was something I hadn't noticed in daily orders.

I got my coffee and headed for the Yard. An ambulance was just moving off from where the man had collapsed as I went by, and the police car had gone.

When I got to my office I phoned a colleague, also a DI and asked him about the masks.

'Haven't you heard,' he said. 'They're part of the uniform from today onwards. There's something going on John. Something strange.'

His words made me think of Clive Price's drunken message and I logged myself out and went home.

It was Dominique's day off and I caught her having coffee with Miriam, one half of the couple who lived next door to us. Miriam and Tom were a little older than us, childless, but always ready to babysit, water the plants when we were away and keep us up to date on local gossip. She didn't work and Tom was a super sales-man for a chemical firm.

'What are you doing here?' Dominique asked. 'Is something wrong?'

'I don't know,' I replied. 'Something's happening certainly, but whether or not it's wrong I don't know.'

I helped myself to coffee, sat at the table and told them what I'd seen earlier. 'Something is up,' said Miriam. 'Tom was due to fly to the States next week, but he's having trouble getting in.'

'What kind of trouble?' I asked.

'They're bringing back the visa laws,' she said.

'What?' I said.

'It's true. He's got to go to the American Embassy and apply in person.'

'I don't believe this,' I said. 'I'm going to phone Clive.'

I went into the living room and called the Foreign Office number from memory and asked to be put through to Clive Price, but was told he was not available. I asked for his secretary and was put through to a woman who told me she was filling in temporarily for Clive's PA who was off sick. I left a message but the call was never returned.

I think around then a lot of calls weren't.

It wouldn't be long before there was no telephone service to return them on.

I went back to the kitchen where the two women had switched on the television. It was tuned into a morning show full of tips about slimming, hair care, bringing up children and cooking, and introduced by a married couple so squeaky clean it was sickening.

That morning the woman was presenting the show alone, claiming sickness in the family as the excuse for her husband's absence.

Suddenly there was a lot of sickness about. Even for February. Even in Great Britain's cold and damp climate.

'What's happening?' said Miriam, looking alarmed as a newsreader with a green tinge to his face came on and reported a flu epidemic across Europe.

'I don't know,' I said although the question hadn't been aimed specifically at me. 'But I intend to find out.'

5

MIRIAM WENT HOME then, and I told Dominique for the first time what Clive had said on the phone. 'Maybe you and Louisa should go somewhere,' I said. 'How about your mother's?' Dominique's mother lived alone near Horsham since her father had died.

'Because of a flu epidemic and one of your friends getting drunk one night and trying to frighten you?'

'I think it might be more than that,' I said.

'I've got work John,' she argued. 'And Louisa's got school.'

'Have you heard anything at work?' I asked. She was employed as a medical researcher at a dental institute in The Strand.

'It's hardly our field,' she replied. 'But I can ask around.'

'And what about Louisa's school?'

'There's a lot of children off with the sniffles, but you know what parents are like these days.'

I did. We were always monitoring Louisa's health and kept her at home much more than I remembered my mother doing with me when I was Louisa's age.

'Listen,' I said. 'I'd better phone in. I'm supposed to be at a meeting after lunch. I just needed to see you were alright.'

'You could have phoned.'

'I know, but I wanted to make sure. I won't be a minute.'

'Go on then,' said Dominique and kissed me. 'You're such a worrier.'

I called in and spoke to my sergeant. 'You'd better come in sir,' he said. 'The Superintendent wants to see everyone.'

'When?'

'One o'clock. I told him you were out on enquiries.'

'Thanks Steve,' I said. 'I'll be back as soon as I can.'

'I've got to go,' I said to Dominique when I joined her again. 'There's a panic on as usual. Better see what it's all about.' And I put my coat back on, kissed my wife again and went out to try and catch a passing cab. There had been a smash on Silvertown

Road and the streets were gridlocked so instead I caught a train up to Victoria again. The station was deserted. There was an ambulance on the forecourt. The paramedics were wearing masks similar to the ones the police officers had been wearing earlier. A railway worker was mopping up the pavement as I passed him and the water in his bucket was tinged with pink.

I walked through the streets to The Yard, and London felt strange. The weight of traffic seemed lighter and the pavements were emptier than normal even for a cold and overcast day. I went to my office where my sergeant, Steve Mortimer was waiting. 'He wants us in there now,' he said. 'What have we done wrong this time?'

'Dunno, but I'm supposed to be at a meeting in ten minutes.'

'Your meeting's cancelled. There's a note on your desk. Someone's sick I think.'

'Who isn't?' I asked and followed him down the corridor to Superintendent Mike Smart's office.

There were several other CID officers present. Mike didn't stand on ceremony and started as soon as we were present. 'These orders come from on high,' he said. 'All leave is cancelled as of now and every available officer is back in uniform.'

'What?' said Detective Inspector Stuart McKinley, close to retirement and in CID for fifteen years. I'd've bet he'd only had his uniform on for promotion ceremonies and funerals in all that time.

'Orders Stu,' said Smart. 'And I'm issuing sidearms.'

There was a general air of disbelief in the room. 'We're about twenty-four hours from a state of emergency being declared. The cabinet's sitting this afternoon in an emergency session. Haven't you lot heard? There's a bloody epidemic going on out there.'

'Mike,' I said. 'There's a few people ill, but isn't this taking things too far?'

'A few people ill,' he came back. 'You lot have been in this ivory tower too long. There's people dying on the streets, don't you know about it?'

'I do,' said Adam Hicks, a DS from Fulham who had been seconded to the Yard recently. 'They're talking about closing my son's school.'

'All school's are closed as from tomorrow,' said Smart. 'There's something bad going on out there and our job's to maintain the Queen's peace. I want you in uniform and in the briefing room in one hour.'

And with that he closed the meeting.

6

THE DEATH came in waves over the next two months. Fast waves and slow waves, and each time that one broke on the beach of human experience we foolishly thought it was to be the last. Thought. Hoped. Prayed. But it was not to be. Our prayers were not answered. God had deserted us in our hour of need, and frankly, after the way we'd treated him over the last two thousand years, who could blame him?

And it was not universally called it The Death. It was also known as The Flu, The Plague, Captain Blood, and any number of other slang names.

The first wave was fast and seemed to take out people with weak immune systems. And they weren't the most obvious victims. Many times we saw grandmothers who seemed to be ready for death themselves nursing their grandchildren who appeared to have the strength of youth on their side. And unfortunately it particularly hurt the emergency services. We lost a lot of police, fire, and medical personnel that first spring of The Death. Too many. And that was when the rioting and looting and killing started.

But I'm getting ahead of myself.

Let's go back to that first afternoon I found myself back in the uniform I kept hanging up in my locker, carrying a Glock nine millimetre seventeen shot semi-automatic pistol in a holster on my waist and sitting in a squad car driven by my closest friend on the force, Sergeant Stephen Mortimer.

It was obvious something bad was happening. The radio was squawking with messages about people collapsing and dying in the streets, offices, tube stations, at bus stops, in shops and cinemas and pubs all over the West End.

We didn't know what the hell was happening. We'd been issued face masks with our guns but I didn't wear mine. I was starting to see so many dead bodies that I figured if my time was up it was up. I was only scared for Dominique and Louisa.

I phoned home from my mobile as we were parked on Vauxhall

Bridge Road around two-thirty. 'The television's gone off,' said Dominique. 'Except Channel Four, and they're showing a film and it should be the news. What's going on?'

'Where's Louisa?' I asked. I wanted to demand, but I didn't want to scare her.

'She's here,' said Dominique. 'I got a call from her headmistress. I went and collected her. The school's shut. I saw some people lying in the street, John, I think they were dead. There was blood…'

'Is she alright?'

'Fine. John, tell me. What's happening?'

'There's some kind of epidemic,' I said looking at Steve sitting next to me in the driver's seat. 'Nobody knows what it is. They've got me back in uniform.' I watched as a figure appeared at the huge doors of the publishers opposite us and clawed at the glass, then slid down coughing blood, which smeared the surface.

Steve immediately called for an ambulance on the car radio.

'I've got to go,' I said to Dominique. 'Keep Louisa indoors. And you stay there too. I'll be home as soon as I can but it may be late. Listen to the radio if there is any. Don't open the door to anyone.'

'I'm frightened John,' she said.

'I am too Dom,' I said. 'But I have to be here. It's my job. Everything will be alright I'm sure. I love you. I'll see you later.'

'I love you too. Be careful.'

'I will,' and I hung up and Steve and I exited the car to go to the aid of the man who'd collapsed, then watched as a car came round the corner from The Embankment too fast, hit the kerb and turned over and over in a kind of slow motion before crashing through the railings that surrounded a small private gardens and came to rest on its roof, wheels spinning, with a plume of smoke coming from the engine bay.

Steve ran towards the wreck but before he could reach it the smoke turned to flame and two explosions ripped through the car making it jump a few inches off the grass where it lay.

I called for fire and more ambulance assistance on my personal radio, but the controller told me that there was at least an hour's delay. I helped Steve fight the flames with the tiny extinguishers we carried in the car but to no avail, and we stood back and watched the fire consume the vehicle and whoever was inside it.

I went across to the publishers but the man who lay half in and half out of the front door was beyond help.

I think it was then that I began to get really scared.

7

I DIDN'T GET HOME until the small hours. Steve dropped me off. It was possibly the worst day I'd ever had on the job. My uniform was torn and stained with blood and worse. We'd ended up at St Thomas's Hospital on the south bank of the Thames opposite the Houses of Parliament. It had been chaos there. People were dead and dying in casualty. All the beds in the hospital had been full since early that morning, and a crowd of sick and injured people had gathered outside with various friends and relations. The roads were packed with cars and ambulances could not get through. Finally we'd had to draw our guns to keep the people from mobbing the hospital. Although no shots had been fired. That was yet to come. Doctors and nurses were working overtime but as so many had succumbed to The Death they were desperately understaffed.

I caught up with a harried looking doctor I'd met before in a rest room on the top floor of the hospital overlooking Westminster. His white coat was filthy, he hadn't shaved, and there was grime in the creases of his face. He was standing, staring at the view, a half-drunk cup of coffee forgotten in his hand. 'You look rough,' I said.

'Evening John,' he replied when he came out of his reverie. 'I feel worse I can tell you.'

'What the hell is going on?' I asked. 'I can't get a word of sense out of anyone.'

'There's no sense to it, that's why,' He replied and dropped into a chair. 'Ever heard of a pandemic John?'

'I think it was an answer in the *Daily Telegraph* crossword once.'

'And that's where it should've stayed. A pandemic is a world wide epidemic. And that's what we have here. I've never seen anything like it before and I doubt if I'll live to see another. The Black Death must've been something like this, except of course they didn't have international travel to spread it like it's spreading now.'

'Is it really that bad?' I asked, a cold lump forming in my stomach.

'Worse. There was a flu epidemic just after the First World War that managed to bump off more people than died in the fighting. But this is even worse than that. We've got bodies piling up in the basement, John, that we haven't even got names for, and my staff are dropping like flies.'

'What about a vaccine?'

'They're trying. God knows they're trying, but this thing whatever it is mutates as fast as we think we've got it licked.'

'Jesus.'

'I think he may be the only one who can help us now,' he said as he got up and put his cup on the table. 'Anyway, I've got to get back. Good luck John, we're going to need it believe me.' And he left. I never saw him again.

Steve and I were finally relieved by a van load of armed police around one a.m. when we managed to fight our way back to our car, which was miraculously undamaged, and got away.

Dominique was waiting up for me. I'd kept in touch with her all day on my mobile. 'You look awful,' she said as I entered the kitchen where she was sitting drinking a cup of tea and I dropped my keys on the table.

'Thanks,' I replied. 'Are you well?'

'No problems,' she said.

'How about Louisa?'

'She's fine. She's asleep. She's so excited about being home from school.'

'Thank God for that,' I said.

'What's the news,' she asked, getting up to put on the kettle.

'God knows,' I said. 'No one's saying anything. At least officially. You probably know more than me.'

'There's no news on the box,' she said. 'Just films and pop videos.'

'The opium of the masses.'

'What's happening John?'

'People are dying. Hundreds, maybe thousands. The emergency

services can't cope. If this carries on I hate to think what's going to happen.'

I took off my gun and holster and put it on the table in front of me.

'Can you put that somewhere safe. I don't want Louisa seeing it.'

'Right now the safest place is with me. I'd be happier if you two went away.'

'What about you?'

'I have a job to do.'

'We're not leaving London without you.'

'I can't go.'

'Then neither can I.'

She was a stubborn woman and I knew better than to argue. 'What about work?' I asked.

'I phoned through. They're closing the labs temporarily. There's a lot of illness. Jack's dead.'

Jack was Dominique's assistant. 'What?' I said.

She started to cry and I went to her. 'Don't, Dom,' I said.

'He was so young.'

'What happened?'

'He caught the sickness. His wife phoned in. He's still at home. She called a doctor but he didn't come. There should be a PM but the mortuaries are full.'

She turned and threw herself into my arms. 'John,' she cried. 'What is happening to the world?'

I wished that I could answer her.

I got a few hours restless sleep with Dominique next to me. I was up by six and tried to get through to the Yard, but the land line was constantly engaged and my mobile refused to work. There was a service on all channels of the television, but only BBC1 and ITV were live. Stern faced individuals on both channels were telling tales of chaos throughout the world. All airports and sea ports were temporarily closed and the body count was in its thousands, although I guessed from what I'd seen that the true figures were being disguised. I went to the local newsagents, which was open, but there were no papers.

When I got back home all I was carrying was a packet of cigarettes, my first for almost five years. I lit one in our tiny garden after Dominique forbade me from smoking indoors.

When I was halfway through the cigarette, which tasted strange and made me feel light-headed, Miriam's husband Tom came into his garden and looked over the fence. 'I thought you didn't,' he said.

'I've started again.'

'That bad?'

'It looks like it.'

'Where did this thing come from John?'

'God knows?'

'On the Internet they're saying it might have something to do with that bomb that went off in Russia last year.'

'I've heard the theory. It's as good as any.'

'I'm stuck. I was supposed to go to New York tomorrow…'

'You're better off here with Miriam.'

'Yes. I can't get through to the office anyway.'

'Nor me.'

'Well if *you* can't…'

Just then Dominique came to the back door. 'Your sergeant's on the phone John,' she said.

'Duty calls,' I said to Tom, grinding my cigarette on the path.

'Let me know what's happening if you can,' he said.

'If I can,' I replied and went inside.

'Steve,' I said when I picked up the receiver from the living room table.

'We're back on duty,' he said. 'I'll come and pick you up. Public transport's a bit dodgy.'

'What's new?'

'Not on the phone sir,' he said. 'I'll fill you in when I get there.'

'That sounds bad.'

'It is. There's been a lot of trouble overnight.'

'Terrific.'

'I'll get to you as quickly as I can.'

'See you then Steve.'

There was a questioning look in Dominique's eyes when I hung up. 'I don't know,' I said. 'But it looks bad.'

8

AND IT WAS BAD. And going to get worse, but how much worse none of us knew.

Steve arrived about an hour later, I'd changed into my spare uniform but hadn't put on my gun because Louisa was up and about and I paid attention to Dominique's request to keep it out of her sight. My sergeant rang the front door bell around eight and I took him into the living room and closed the door behind us. 'Exactly what's happening?' I asked. 'I can't get through to the Yard.'

'I slept up there,' he said. 'For once I'm glad I've got no family. It's like the Third World War out there.'

'Tell me the worst.'

'I suppose you know that most businesses are temporarily closed,' he said.

'That was on the news.'

'Yeah, but the news people don't know the half of it.'

'Like what?'

'Like the fact that the Prime Minister is dead.'

'Are you serious?'

He nodded. 'It happened last night. Smith's the new PM. He'll be making an announcement on all television channels at noon.'

'Jesus,' I said.

'And there's rioting up north. People trying to get into hospital. The centre of Manchester is in flames.'

'There was nothing about that on the news.'

'The cabinet's brought back 'D' Notices. From now on it's just the news we want them to tell.'

'How many are really dead?'

'No one knows. At least a quarter of a million it's estimated.'

'That many?'

'At least. And it's worse in America.'

I thought about my doctor friend. 'What about the medical authorities? What the hell is it Steve?'

'Some kind of flu based botulism is the best guess. It comes on fast and is fatal. Sometimes there's severe haemorrhaging, sometimes not.'

I was more or less thinking aloud. 'And there's no antidote?'

'Not so far. Believe me they're working on it.'

'I heard. I was talking to someone at Tommy's last night. But the damn thing keeps mutating, according to him.'

'That's what they told me too. A lot of people think it's man made.'

'And a lot of people might be right. Science has come up with some nasty stuff in the last few years.'

'Well this looks like the nastiest.'

'And what about us?'

'We've got a roving assignment. We just go when and where we're wanted.'

'I told Dominique to get out of London.'

'It doesn't seem to make any difference. The country's as badly hit as the towns. And besides there's chaos on the roads out of London. They've closed the motorways because there've been so many accidents.'

'My God. Is this the end?'

'We don't know John, we really don't, but unless something happens soon it seems like we're looking at anarchy.'

'I hate to leave Dominique and Louisa alone.'

'John, listen,' he said. 'I don't blame you, but someone's got to keep order out there. People are scared shitless. If we shirk our responsibility, God knows what will happen. At the moment the streets are quiet, the army's ready to mobilise if there's more riots. Do you want to see soldiers on the streets? Come up to the Yard. Speak to the Super.'

I was wracked with doubt. I knew what he said was true but I was terrified for my family. 'OK Steve.' I said. 'But I don't like it.'

'No one does.'

I went back to where Dominique was giving Louisa her breakfast. 'I'm going to go,' I said. 'I have to.'

'I know,' she replied.

'I'll try and keep in touch.'

'I still can't get through to mum,' she said.

'Keep trying,' I said. For the first time ever I was glad my mother and father were dead and I was an only child.

'I will.'

And with that I kissed her and Louisa goodbye, strapped on my gun under the watchful eye of Steve and left the house.

9

WHETHER I KNEW IT OR NOT that was going to be my last day at work. My last day as a copper, because that was the day that the shit hit the fan and it all fell apart. It didn't take much. Civilisation was a delicate flower that curled up and died with a speed that no one could forsee and chaos followed swiftly.

Not that some people didn't try and keep it going. Some dedicated citizens who tried to keep the lamps burning. Literally in the cases of the gas and electricity workers. But it was only a matter of a few days before the barbarians who'd been waiting in the wings for their chance took over, and those who'd elected to try and sustain the old ways died in their attempts.

Steve went that morning.

We'd driven over the river from my house to Scotland Yard where faceless men in blue overalls carrying submachine guns guarded the exits and entrances.

We found a parking space and went looking for Superintendent Smart. He was in the sick bay coughing blood. 'Keep away boys,' he said with a rictus. 'Looks like I've got it. I don't want either of you dying because of me.'

Even then, after Susan no-last-name I had a feeling that I was not going to get sick. 'Don't worry Boss,' I said. 'You'll be OK.'

'I doubt it John,' he replied. 'This isn't just a chill I've got here.'

'What do you want us to do?' I asked.

He sighed. 'What can you do? I've been up all night watching things on the closed circuit. It's fucked out there and it's going to get worse.' He coughed and pink liquid splashed down his uniform shirt and he grabbed the back of a chair for support.

I went to him but he pushed me back. 'Think of your family John,' he said.

'What about yours?' I asked.

Tears came to his eyes. 'Marjorie died yesterday. Kate's up at Hull Uni. But you know that John. I've heard nothing.'

'I'm sorry Mike,' I said using his Christian name for the first time.

'Get the hell out of here,' he said. 'You too Steve. Go and look after your own.' And he sat down and put his head in his hands and started to cry.

I looked at Steve. 'Come on mate,' I said. 'Let's go see what we can see.'

When we got back to the car I said. 'You don't have to work Steve. Not if you don't want to.'

'Nor do you.'

'I'm here aren't I? Might as well take a drive round, check out the area.'

'What about Dominique and Louisa?'

'They'll be OK. You were right Steve; we've got a duty. That's what we signed on for.'

That was probably the most stupid thing I've ever said in my life.

'If you're going I'm coming too,' he said.

And with those few words he signed his own death warrant.

10

THEY LAID THE AMBUSH for us in a narrow street in Battersea. We got a call over the radio to go to the scene of a disturbance. As Steve steered the car carefully between a couple of burnt out vehicles, one car swung across the front of us and another skidded to a halt at the back. Then a bunch of people, men, women and children, appeared as if from nowhere, armed with sticks and baseball bats and surrounded our car. Many of them looked ill with runny noses and coughs that racked their bodies. Some were so far gone that they were bleeding from every pore. It was a truly horrifying sight. One woman was carrying a child in her arms. I was sure it was dead. 'Shit,' said Steve.

I opened the door my side and stood, using it as a shield. 'You people,' I said to the crowd. 'Move those cars and then yourselves.'

'Bollocks,' said a big man carrying a stave.

'Watch it, he's got a gun,' said the woman by his side who had a halfbrick in her fist.

'We both have,' I said.

'Give us the car,' said the man.

'What do you want the car for?' I asked. 'There's hundreds of cars around. Take your pick.'

'It's got a radio and machine guns,' said the man with the stave.

'This isn't armed response,' I said. 'It's just a regular squad car.'

'Why you got a gun then?' said the man.

'That's neither here nor there. Now do us a favour and move. We've got a job to do.'

I'd heard Steve calling in on the radio whilst I spoke and then he joined me, standing on the far side of the car. 'We're expecting backup.' he said.

'Backup,' said the woman. 'Haven't you heard, you cunt? This

39

is the end of the world.' And she threw a brick that hit Steve on the side of the head.

'That was stupid,' I said. 'Are you OK Steve?'

He was white faced and his skin was split and already beginning to bruise, but he managed to nod as he put his hand up to his head.

'OK,' I said. 'I know you're scared. We all are. But if you'll just move we'll forget all this happened.'

'No,' said a voice from the back of the crowd and it parted to allow a man through carrying a double barrelled shotgun.

'Put it away,' I said. 'This is crazy. We're all in the same boat here.'

'No we're not,' he said. 'You're in charge just like always. Or at least you think you are. But times have changed. We're in charge now. So just leave us the car and your guns. Then you can go. We've got no argument with you.'

'I have,' said the woman. 'Those bastards put my Phil away.'

'Shut up Sue,' said the man with the shotgun. 'We've heard it all before.'

'We can't,' I said. 'We're still the law.'

'That's a fucking laugh,' said the man with the shotgun. 'There is no law anymore. Take your guns out, put them on the car and walk away. Or I'll kill you.'

I looked at Steve who was standing with his hand against his forehead, blood leaking between his fingers.

'Now,' pressed the man and he gestured with the gun whose barrels looked as big as railway tunnels.

Steve took his hand away from his wound, reached down, unsnapped the retaining strap over the hammer of his Glock and gingerly, with two fingers, pulled the gun from its holster.

Damn, I thought and did the same, all the time keeping my eyes on the face of the man with the shotgun whose eyes flicked back and forth between us.

The crowd leant forward and as the man looked at me, Steve fumbled his pistol into his hand and raised it to fire.

The man with the shotgun took his eyes off me and fired at

Steve tearing a bloody hole in his chest and splashing the side of the squad car with cloth from his jacket, blood and bone splinters.

It gave me the second I needed to bring my gun into play and I fired three rapid shots. The first tore into the man with the shotgun's neck and went on to hit a black woman, who was standing beside, him between the eyes. The second hit him in the chest and the third caught the woman he'd called Sue in the cheek and blew the back of her head off.

The man with the shotgun looked amazed at what had happened, stepped back, tripped on the kerb, fell back against the black woman and they both tumbled to the ground when by reflex he fired the second barrel of his gun harmlessly into the air.

It was the first time I'd fired my gun in anger and I felt sick at the carnage, but swung the barrel round at the crowd. 'Who's next?' I shouted above the ringing of the five shots in my ears. 'Which one of you bastards wants the next? I've got plenty of bullets left.'

I looked over at Steve who was leaning against the car his gun still in his hand. He turned painfully towards me and said 'Good shooting John.' And when I looked at the crowd again it was already beginning to disperse, leaving its dead behind in the gutter.

I WAS SHAKING as I managed to get Steve into the back of the car and laid him on the seat. He was losing blood heavily and my hands were red with gore. 'Is anyone coming?' I said. 'Where are they?'

'No one's coming John,' he replied in a whisper. 'The radio's gone. I was talking to dead air. Bluffing. It's over John.'

'Don't worry Steve,' I said. 'You'll be alright. Trust me.'

I got into the driver's seat, put the squad car into gear and pushed the car that had pulled in front of us out of the way, and with a screech of metal forced my vehicle through the gap I'd made, feeling a wheel run over the body of one of our ambushers as we went, and headed for St Thomas's, which was the nearest hospital.

'We'll be there soon,' I said as I accelerated.

Steve died on the way, giving a terrible moan as he rolled off the seat onto the floor behind me. 'We're fucked,' were his last words.

I stopped the car and went to his assistance but it was too late. I sat with my friend for five minutes on the embankment of the River Thames holding his hand with one of mine until it began to cool. In my other hand I held his Glock with the hammer back and my finger on the trigger, but all I saw were army trucks in a convoy speeding past towards the centre of London. The streets were quiet.

I knew what he'd said with his dying words was true and I turned the car in the direction of Chelsea Police Station, which was the closest. Outside the nick there were the bodies of civilians and police personnel on the pavement, and inside the building there were more dead casualties. There'd been a recent fire fight and the floors were sticky with drying blood. The station was deserted and had been ransacked, and I carried my gun in my hand as I prowled the empty corridors looking for some sign of life, but found none.

I drove Steve's body through empty streets back home and when I was parked outside I called Dominique on my mobile which mercifully was working and told her there'd been some trouble, that I was alright and that she should get Louisa upstairs so that she couldn't see the state of me.

I gave it a couple of minutes, then let myself in. Dominique was waiting and covered her mouth to silence a scream at the sight of the blood on my clothes. 'It's alright,' I explained. 'I'm OK.'

'What happened?'

I told her.

'Poor Steve,' she said.

'Poor everyone,' I said back.

I took off my clothes and put them into a garbage bag and went upstairs for a shower but the water was off and I made do with rinsing myself with cold water from the tank in the loft that we were keeping to drink.

'Where is he?' Dominique asked when I joined her in the kitchen.

'In the car.'

'Isn't there somewhere you can take him?'

I told her about Chelsea Police Station. 'There is nowhere Dom,' I said. 'It's buggered out there. Finished.'

'But it's been so quick,' she said.

'We were too civilised. We relied too much on other people. Gas, water, electric. We took it all for granted for too long and now it's broken down and we don't know what to do.'

'What are we going to do?'

'God knows. Try and get out of London if they'll let us. Have you spoken to your mother?'

'Not for days. Her phone's dead. She said she felt sick. I'm scared she's dead.'

'Oh Dominique,' I said. 'We could try and get to her. But the roads…They've closed the motorways and brought in the army, but people are getting sick so quickly I don't know what's going to happen next.'

'Are you going back to work?'

'No. There is no work. I shouldn't've gone out this morning.'

'What about Steve's body?'

'I'll bury it in the garden. He had no family.'

'Isn't that against the law?'

I almost laughed, but it would have been too gruesome. 'What law?' I said. 'I'm the law. You're the law. We're all the law now and look what's happening.'

Dominique helped me carry Steve's body through the house and I dug a shallow grave and laid him to rest with a few words from the Bible that we only occasionally opened.

The end of the world had come and I didn't know what to do.

But worse. Much worse was to follow.

12

DOMINIQUE AND LOUISA contracted The Death two days later. In my ignorance I was convinced that all three of us were immune, and that the angel of death would pass over our house, but I was wrong.

Dominique was the first to show any symptoms.

By then we'd settled into a sort of routine. Martial law had been declared and the BBC and commercial radio and the utility companies had been taken over by the military. By listening to our battery radio to the one London station still broadcasting on FM we were informed when we could expect gas, electricity and water services to be resumed in our area. That morning there was electricity between nine and ten a.m., and we were toasting stale bread and making black tea for breakfast when she sneezed. 'What's the matter?' I said.

'Nothing. Just a sniffle.'

'Dominique.'

'It's nothing I tell you. I always get a cold at this time of the year. You know that.' But I could see by her eyes that she was terrified.

I swallowed the lump in my throat and said. 'That'll be it.' But I knew it wasn't and there was nothing I could do.

Her symptoms got worse as the morning went on and I insisted that she go back to bed whilst I scouted around for food. The truth was I couldn't bear to think of her getting ill and I had to get away and think.

I went to the supermarket but it was closed and I walked the streets looking for something, anything to replenish our shrinking larder. Finally I found a corner shop that was open and guarded by armed solders. I joined the queue that stretched for yards along the pavement and must have been at least fifty strong.

'It ain't fair,' said an elderly woman in front of me to her friend. 'My husband fought for this country and now I can't even bury him proper.'

'Where is he?' her friend asked.

'In the back bedroom. The smell's something terrible but no one will do anything.'

'The soldiers'll come for him,' said her friend. 'They're driving round in dust carts picking up the dead.'

It was amazing to me how quickly we were adapting.

'I don't like the thought,' said the first woman. 'Not putting him out with the rubbish.'

'But you've got to do something with him.'

'I know. Do you think this'll ever end?'

'God knows,' said the second woman. 'I thought we'd seen it all in the Blitz.'

'This is worse,' said the first woman. 'And I'm missing *Coronation Street*. I can't get a bloody thing on my telly.'

'So much for all that digital rubbish,' the second woman opined.

Their conversation was interrupted when one of the young soldiers fell to his knees vomiting blood. 'Christ,' said the first woman. 'He's got it too.'

The other soldier, a young man barely out of his teens dropped his rifle and went to his friend's aid, which was a signal for the queue to fragment, join together again and burst through the narrow door of the shop intent on getting their hands on anything eatable inside, and to my shame I joined them. The shopkeeper was an Asian and he was knocked to the ground as he tried to protect his depleted stock. The place was chaotic, lit only by candles; it was a nightmare scene as people fought for anything they could grab, their shadows dancing across the emptying shelves.

I managed to procure two small tins of beans and a head of lettuce that was almost black with rot before the young soldier picked up his rifle and fired into the air.

The mob froze, then one middle aged man who had been unable to force his way into the shop began to wrestle with the soldier. Suddenly an armoured car came round the corner and three more armed soldiers leapt out. I could see serious trouble starting and I ran back out of the door and down the side street away from the scene as an officer put his revolver to the middle aged man's head and shot him at point blank range.

'Stop or I'll shoot,' he shouted at me but I dived into someone's front garden, clambered over the back gate, pelted across the lawn and over another fence. I lay trembling with my back to it as I heard screams and shots from behind me.

I hid there for five minutes in the cover of a privet hedge before I dared move. The house whose garden I was in was dark and quiet, and I let myself through to the front and into the parallel street and made my way home, my looted treasures safe in the pockets of my coat.

Dominique was worse when I got back, and Louisa was coughing blood just like the soldier had.

13

I CALLED OUT Dominique's name when I got indoors as I took the food to the kitchen.

She answered my shout from upstairs where I found her sitting by Louisa's bed wiping the pink drool from her chin. They both looked as bad as each other and my heart lurched in my chest. I couldn't lose them. Not the only people I was living for. Please God, don't let that happen, I thought. But God was dead, or asleep. Or he just didn't care.

'Daddy,' my little girl said plaintively. 'I don't feel well.'

'I know darling,' I said bending to kiss her hot and sweaty brow. 'But you'll feel better soon I promise.'

It was an empty promise at best, a lie at worst, and both Dominique and I knew it.

'Try and get some sleep sweetheart,' I said. 'I need to talk to mummy. We'll be back soon.'

'I want a hot drink daddy,' said Louisa.

I looked at my watch. It was nearly noon by then and I knew the electricity was off for the rest of the day. 'We'll see what we can do,' I said. 'Dom, let's see what we can find.'

Dominique kissed Louisa too, got up, stumbled, and I grabbed her and led her out of the room.

'I'm bad,' she said when we were on the landing and the door was closed behind us. 'So's Lou. John I'm terrified.'

'I know,' I said. 'Let me get you to bed.'

'Bed's no good. I'm dying,' and she started a racking cough and blood seeped out of her nose.

'Dom,' I said. 'You won't die if I have anything to do with it.'

'But you don't,' she replied and fell against me and I half dragged, half carried her to our bedroom and laid her on the unmade bed. 'And there's no hot water for Lou's drink,' she wailed as I undressed her and pulled the covers up to her chin.

'I'll go and see Miriam and Tom,' I said. 'They might have some in a flask or in the kettle or something.'

'Look after Louisa, John,' she said. 'Promise me that.'

'I'll look after both of you,' I said. 'Just give me a minute and I'll be back.'

I went downstairs, out of the front door and into our neighbours' front garden and knocked on the door. This time I took my gun. There were soldiers out there shooting to kill, and I'd kill them before they stopped me caring for my family.

There was no answer next door for so long that I checked to see if Tom and Miriam's cars were parked outside. They were. Shit, I thought, not them too, and went back and hammered at the wood. The door opened and Miriam appeared wearing a dirty white night dress that was covered in dried blood.

'Get away John,' she said through a mouthful of mucus. 'We've got it. You'll catch it.' and she fell into my arms.

I lifted her and carried her back inside and slammed the door behind me. The house stank of bodily matter and I called Tom's name but got no reply. I took Miriam into her lounge and laid her on the sofa and went looking for her husband. He was upstairs in bed. Next to the bed was a bucket of blood and faeces. I checked his pulse. It was weak but he was still alive. There was nothing I could do except leave them there. I found a blanket to cover Miriam. On the way out of the house I checked the kitchen which was a mess. There was no hot water anywhere to be found.

I stood in the hall deliberating what to do, but there was nothing.

With what felt like the weight of the world on my shoulders I went back to my wife and child.

Dominique was in a coma when I got back to our bedroom so I left her. There was no alternative. Louisa was burning up but at least she was awake. She had thrown the bedclothes off and I sat and held her hand until she too fell asleep. She was too weak to speak.

The day had flown by and it was nearly dark by then, and I went down to our living room after checking on Dominique whose condition hadn't changed, and found a half empty bottle of whisky and sat looking out at the black and deserted street from our front window and wondered how the hell this was all going to end.

BY THE NEXT MORNING Dominique and Louisa were both dead, and I knelt by their beds and cried and cursed God and man and myself for allowing it to happen. I went next door to Tom and Miriam's but there was no answer to my relentless knocking, so I smashed the window beside the front door and let myself in. Somehow during the night Miriam had dragged herself upstairs to die beside her husband and I covered their bodies with a counterpane and left them.

I went back to my house and into the garden where someone or something, whether it was man or beast I know not had been at Steve's grave, and I saw his hand sticking up through the dirt. That was almost the last straw, and I came close to losing my mind at the sight of it, and I howled at the fates and screamed for vengeance, but no one heard.

I picked up my spade and dug a grave next to his for my girls. I brought them down wrapped in blankets and laid them together, then smashed down the fence into Tom and Miriam's garden where they had been building a patio before The Death came and lugged back enough bricks to cover the last resting place of Steve and my beloved's so that nothing else could dig them up.

When I was finished I tried to think of some words to say over their graves but none would come.

It would be a long time before I would speak again.

I went back inside and the electricity was on again and I made myself a cup of coffee and found some dry biscuits to eat. I hadn't touched food for over twenty-four hours and I was ravenous.

I think it was then that I realised that I was definitely immune to The Death and that was the final black joke that almost drove me to use my own gun on myself and finish my life there and then.

But I didn't. Instead I found a haversack in the loft, filled it with some clothes and toilet things and left our house where we'd been so happy, for the last time, and, abandoning my own car and the squad car I walked in the direction of the River Thames, never once looking back over my shoulder.

I WOKE UP back in the real world with tears drying on my face. It was full night, clouds scudded across the sky and when they obliterated the moon it was as black as pitch. The fire had died to embers and Ugly was snoring like a buzzsaw. That wasn't what had woken me. I was used to his noises.

It was Puppy. She had crept up close to me and I could feel her warm breath on my cheek. She was trying to tell me something. I held her snout closed, lay very still and pricked my ears. Then I heard it again. Somewhere back in the undergrowth on the other side of the fire close to where Ugly was sleeping something or someone was moving. The moon appeared again and lit the clearing like day, then just as quickly it was obscured again and I grabbed the Winchester which I kept by my side wherever I slept, rolled under the branches of a bush as silently as I knew how, leaving Puppy with a tap on her nose. She knew that meant to stay still and quiet whatever happened.

I heard the sound again and I rose and slid backwards until I was completely under cover.

The clouds moved on and the clearing appeared before me again and two figures moved stealthily out of the copse we'd camped next to. They were scruffy and dirty, looking like they'd been on the road for a long time. One knelt beside Ugly and put a blade to his throat as the other kicked life into the fire. 'Hey Piggy,' said the man with the knife. 'Wake up.'

Piggy. That was nice. I'm sure Ugly would appreciate that. I'd have to remind him. As often as possible. I moved round quietly so that all three would be silhouetted by the dim light from the fire.

Ugly came awake with a grunt as he felt the steel on his skin. 'That truck yours?' said the man with the knife.

Ugly nodded as much as possible without cutting his own throat. 'Keys?'

'Pocket,' said Ugly.

'Get 'em Ray,' said the knifeman.

I stepped out of the bushes as Ray began to make a move on Ugly. 'Don't,' I said.

Ray went for something in his pocket and I blew his chest through his backbone and he crashed back onto the fire.

'Put down the knife arsehole,' I said to the other one.

Ugly didn't give him a chance. He reached up with one bear-like paw and snatched the blade, then came to his feet with more grace than most would've given him credit for and stood behind his assailant.

'Hey man,' the knifeman said to me. 'We were only kidding. You didn't need to kill Ray. We just needed a lift. We've been walking for days.'

'Someone steal your car?' I asked.

'No. We had horses. They got spooked and ran off.'

'Too bad,' I said. 'You should've just kept on walking, Felix.'

He looked confused in the light of the moon. Maybe he'd never seen the cartoons.

'Listen,' he said. 'You've got stuff to trade on board your truck. I know a place just down the road. They pay in gold and guns and ammo and women. Prime stuff.'

'Where down the road?' grunted Ugly.

'Bout thirty miles. Just outside Cambridge on the old Cambridge Road. They've got electricity and booze. It's a pub.'

'We'll find it,' I said.

'But you'll need me for introduction.'

'If they're traders what we've got will be introduction enough.'

'No man. Take me along. They like me there.'

'We don't like you here,' I said.

'So what are you going to do?'

'Kill you,' I replied. 'Like your pal there, slow cooking on the barbecue.'

'No,' said the knifeman. 'No. Please.'

Ugly moved to one side.

'Go on then, fuck off,' I said.

The knife man sighed with relief and turned to walk out of the clearing and I shot him in the back, the load knocking him face down in the dirt.

Ugly went and knelt beside him. 'He's still alive,' he said in a disappointed voice.

I joined him and finished the knifeman with a shot in the back of the head with my .38.

'Three shells to kill two,' said Ugly. 'You're slipping.'

'Search them,' I said. 'And mind out. The way that fucker in the fire's burning if he's got any bullets on him they could pop off in your face.'

Ugly pulled Ray out of the fire but all he found on him was a torch with a weak battery. The knifeman had his knife and a .38 revolver. It was empty and Ugly chucked it into the back of the truck. It was just as well he'd run out of ammunition as he'd probably have killed my friend with a single bullet and asked no questions. I didn't bother to go into that. Ugly would've only got upset.

It was enough as it was. 'What took you so long?' Ugly demanded after he'd made up the fire and started some water for coffee. 'That bastard could've cut my throat in my sleep.'

'No Piggy,' I said. 'He wanted to fuck you up the arse first. Probably kill you as he came. I heard it's good when that happens. Just like in that film *Deliverance*. Remember that one?'

'I remember.'

'That was probably his favourite film,' I said. 'He looked like he might play the banjo too.'

'You're becoming a real charmer, John,' said Ugly.

'I try and get better every day,' I said. 'And don't thank me, thank Puppy. It was her that woke me up.'

'Good dog,' said Ugly and he ruffled her coat.

'And when it gets light let's head down the Cambridge Road and check out that place he told us about,' I said. 'See if we can do some business.'

'Suits me,' said Ugly. 'And John.'

'Yeah.'

'Don't ever let me hear you call me Piggy again.'

'I'll try and remember,' I said.

THE SUN ROSE EARLY and we left the two dead bodies in the clearing for worm food and drove off at around seven.

The roads weren't bad. Most of the vehicles which had been abandoned during the panicky rush after The Death arrived, some still containing the skeletal remains of their drivers and passengers who'd been struck down en-route, having been stripped and cleared by earlier travellers. But still occasionally we came across fallen trees or the remains of barricades built by the locals in a fruitless attempt to keep their little corners of the world free from the plague victims and the infection they carried, until they realised that quarantine was fruitless and they either died or left themselves, and we had to use the Land Rover's winch to clear a way or else go cross country using the 4WD.

We passed through several deserted villages which, only months after The Death had come already showed signs of neglect and the onslaught of nature. I wondered how long it would be before they decayed back into the countryside where they'd been born hundreds, even thousands of years before.

The major signs of life we saw as we drove through the morning that was already becoming unbearably hot, were foxes, deer and a couple of packs of wild dogs. These were becoming a major nuisance and one pack ran beside our truck and Puppy pressed her nose against the window as she watched them. 'Stay girl,' I said and she turned her liquid eyes to me, which were filled with a longing to be amongst her own kind. 'Bloody dogs,' I said.

'If we had more ammo we could cull the bleeders,' said Ugly.

'Something'll have to be done soon,' I replied.

'You sound like the local council,' he said.

'Funny. Christ I wish we'd got a Range Rover with air conditioning. This heat's doing my head in.'

'Poof's car,' said Ugly disparagingly. 'Alright for the weekly run to Sainsbury's, when there was a Sainsbury's, but no good to us. Air conditioning uses up too much fuel. And we need the winch.'

'Police Range Rovers had winches,' I said wistfully as I lit a cigarette.

'Yeah. But we haven't seen one. If we do…'

'Promises, promises,' I said and wiped my face on my sleeve.

We stopped around noon to eat on the top of a hill and I checked the map as we lounged in the shade and ate cold beans straight from the tin and Puppy tucked into a tin of Fido. 'The old Cambridge Road runs down there,' I said, pointing west. 'I reckon we should check out that place your boyfriend told us about.'

'If it exists,' said Ugly. 'And he wasn't my boyfriend.'

'I reckon he wanted to be though.'

'He was probably lying to stay alive a bit longer.'

'Didn't work, did it?' I said. 'And if it's true what he said about them having ammunition to trade…'

'It's worth a look,' my friend said as he sucked at a warm bottle of beer. 'But don't hold your breath.'

That was when we heard the sound of engines, full throated and deep coming from the direction that I'd pointed.

'What the fuck is that?' said Ugly.

'Sounds like motorbikes to me,' I replied and slid my Glock from its holster.

Ugly looked at the gun. 'Don't get excited,' he said. 'They're miles away.'

'And getting closer,' I pointed out.

'I reckon they're on the Cambridge Road too,' he said.

'I wonder where they could be going?' I said to myself as much as to him.

'Same place as us I imagine. Maybe that evil little fucker was telling the truth. Beer and women remember.'

'And fucking bikers. That's the last thing we need.'

'I eat bikers for breakfast,' said Ugly.

'Well you might have your chance,' I told him. 'Sooner than

you think.'

The sound of engines grew then faded as they passed by below us. 'Yep,' said Ugly. 'Sounds like a party.'

'Want to go?' I asked him.

'Haven't been to a party in months.'

'Then let's see if we're invited.'

WE GOT INTO THE TRUCK and drove down the hill until we came to the main road. Someone had done a good job of completely clearing it, and the fields and woods at the side were full of cars that had been pushed off the road so that both sides were graveyards of crushed metal. 'Someone used a bulldozer here,' said Ugly, pointing out the scars from caterpillar tracks that were still visible on the verges of the road.

'Very professional,' I agreed as we drove slowly along the metalled tarmac in the direction that the motorbikes had taken.

After a few miles the road rose sharply and when we hit the brow of the hill we looked down onto a small village with a big old roadhouse pub at a crossroads. The road that crossed ours then spanned a narrow, fast running river on our right by an old brick bridge before running out of sight into some woods. The river itself ran along the back of the pub forming a natural moat between it and the same woods.

From the direction of the pub came sounds that I hadn't heard for months, since before The Death struck.

Ugly braked the Land Rover and said 'What's that?'

'Turn off the engine,' I said and when he did we could clearly hear the sound of loud music from below.

'Jesus,' said Ugly. 'Steppenwolf. *Born To be Wild.*'

I looked round and saw a narrow walled lane leading off to our right. 'Go back,' I said. 'Drive up there.'

Ugly started the engine, reversed the truck down past the entrance to the lane that wasn't blocked by wrecked cars, and steered the Land Rover into it. We drove down about three hundred yards and came to a lay-by shielded by trees. 'In there,' I said.

Ugly drove into the lay-by and parked in the shade. 'Come on let's have a squint. Bring the bins.'

In the glove compartment he found our pair of very powerful, very expensive binoculars that we'd liberated from the cabin of a millionaire's cruiser that had gone aground on the Thames just after we'd first met, and leaving Puppy in the truck we set off in the direction of the village cross country, following our ears, as the music, which was now *Light My Fire* by The Doors, continued blasting out.

We reached the brow of the hill again and found a clear view and lay in the grass and Ugly passed me the field glasses and I zoomed in on the building.

It was massive, probably built in the twenties or thirties and now converted into a semi-fortress.

The pub itself was set in the middle of a huge car park next to an old fashioned wooden barn of a garage with two primitive petrol pumps in front of it, one bearing an old Shell sign and the other an equally ancient BP top. The wall round the car park had been strengthened with wood topped with barbed wire and a chain link fence had been built to separate it into two halves. Inside the far half, next to the garage, were parked two petrol tankers close up to a large lean-to coming from which, when the music stopped between records, we could clearly hear the sound of a powerful generator which obviously supplied electricity to the complex. Behind the lean-to, painted a distinct yellow were a bulldozer and a JCB earth mover with a massive mechanical shovel mounted on the front. Obviously these were the machines that had been used to clear the road.

The pub itself, which from this angle we could see had extensive outbuildings at its back, had been fortified with wooden shutters over the windows and someone had climbed onto the covered veranda that ran round the three sides of the pub that we could see and written in white paint THE LAST CHANCE SALOON in letters three feet high on the brickwork above the front door. All round the building, connected by wire, were hundreds of coloured bulbs.

In the front part of the car park seven gleaming motorcycles all chopped into hogs were parked in a neat row alongside several high powered saloon cars, three pickup trucks on huge tyres and a Range Rover.

'Bloody hell,' I said to Ugly, passing him the bins. 'Take a look at that, won't you.'

He put the instruments to his eyes and scrutinised the building, then lowered them, spat into the grass, wiped his mouth with the back of his hand and said. 'Heavy. Did you see what was written on the blackboard by the door?'

No,' I replied and he passed the binoculars back and I looked where he pointed.

On a big blackboard in coloured chalk was written:

THE LAST CHANCE
BEER WINE WHISKEY FOOD
DEALS DONE
NO FIREARMS
EVERY NITE WET T-SHIRT COMPETITION 10PM
WOMEN TO RENT
ALL WELCOME

'Now how did I miss that?' I said.

Whilst I was looking, a big man in jeans and a white vest came out of the front door of the pub carrying a stubby Heckler & Koch MP5K 9mm automatic personal defence weapon with a short magazine that carried thirty rounds. 'So much for no firearms,' I said, pointing it out to Ugly. 'They must have some ammunition down there. And boy I would dearly love one of those H&Ks. I trained with them years ago, you know.'

'So let's go and have a look,' said Ugly.

'I don't like those bikes.'

'So we wait 'til later. 'Til it gets dark. Maybe they'll be gone by then. Or too drunk to see straight.'

'OK.'

'Deals done,' said Ugly.

'That's our game.'

'Wet T-shirt competition.' Ugly again.

'I thought you'd like that.'

'Ten tonight.'

'So we'll go then.'

'No firearms.'

'We'll leave our carry weapons in the truck and leave the truck out of sight. I don't fancy losing the lot.'

'Not that we would.'

'They don't know that. They might just try.'

'We'd soon show them different.'

'Course we would.'

And with that we moved back down the hill on our hands and knees until we were out of sight of the pub and we could walk upright back to the Land Rover.

WHEN WE GOT BACK to the truck we rolled it further out of sight under the trees and I left Ugly snoozing in the driver's seat whilst I took Puppy with me and went to check the abandoned cars to see if there was anything worth salvaging.

But we'd been beaten to it. They'd been stripped down to bare metal and after a while I gave up and found a shady spot and sat down with my back to a tree and lit a cigarette. When Puppy realised I wasn't moving she spun round in a clump of soft grass and went to sleep with one eye shut and the other on me in case I abandoned her.

She'd never learn.

I'd never leave her. Not after all that we'd been through together.

I stretched my legs out in front of me and thought back to those first days after Dominique and Louisa had died and how close I came to dying myself.

I walked the streets the morning that I'd buried my wife and daughter and it was only then that I began to understand the enormity of the blight that had fallen upon the world.

The city was silent. As silent as I'd ever known it and I'd lived there all my life.

But things were happening. I could tell that. I could feel I was being watched as I walked, spied on by dozens of invisible eyes, and over all hung a pall of smoke as buildings burned all over town. But no sirens heralded fire engines racing to put out the fires.

Pudding Lane to Pie Corner. Some of my history came back to me. This looked like it had the makings of the third great fire of London. The first in 1666, strangely enough after another plague had ravaged the city. The second in the forties when Hitler tried to bomb us out of existence. And now, by accident or design, the third one. And once this one really took hold it wouldn't stop until it burnt itself out.

I headed for Victoria. I don't know if it was to go to the Yard or to the railway station where when I was a kid I'd been taken on day trips to Brighton, some of my happiest memories. God knows what I was thinking. I'd just lost the only people who meant anything to me and I think I was a little crazy.

I crossed the Thames at Vauxhall, and looking down river, for a moment I imagined that everything was back to normal so ordinary was the sight, until I spotted several bodies floating in the water, almost looking like they were waving to me as the tidal stream took them. I went down the Vauxhall Bridge Road which was deserted except for abandoned vehicles which littered the streets and stretched as far as the eye could see, when the brick wall beside me exploded in a cloud of dust. Seconds after the sound of a shot echoed through the empty canyon of the street.

Jesus, I thought as I instinctively fell to the pavement, drew the Glock from under my arm and rolled under a car that was half off, half on, the pavement. Snipers. Just what I wanted.

I poked my head from under the car's chassis and another bullet smacked into the metalwork above me followed by the sound of the report that told me whoever was shooting was a fair distance away. Probably in one of the blocks on the east side of the street opposite the theatre.

I crawled back and lay still and checked what options I could see from my position. There was no point in trying to return fire. The shooter obviously had a rifle and I'd just be wasting ammo. I looked round desperately. Next to where I was lying was a low fence, a stretch of grass, then the entrance to a block of flats which was part of a low-rise estate that ran down most of one side of the road. That looked like the best chance to get out of the sniper's field of fire because I'd walked through the flats many times and the walkways were a maze.

I rolled out from under the car, came to my feet, jumped the fence and zigzagged across the grass as bullets tore up the turf beside me. But whoever was shooting wasn't up to much, and within seconds I was between two high walls and safe as the skies opened and it began to pour with rain.

That was the last time I walked down a London street in plain sight.

But it wasn't going to be the end of my troubles for the day.

19

I WAS SOON SOAKED to the skin and I'd lost my bag of clothes when I'd been ambushed by the anonymous sniper, so all I had left were my two Glocks, my cigarettes and lighter and what I stood up in. It was almost like being born again, so I just shrugged to myself and kept heading for Victoria, dodging from doorway to doorway, using back streets only, and as I got closer I began to notice a foul smell permeating the air.

It was thick and pungent and I recognised it as something I'd encountered many times before in my career as a policeman. It was the smell of death. The smell of decaying flesh. But previously it had mostly been localised inside closed doors as some poor sod rotted away after being brutally murdered, or someone had died alone and not been missed for weeks and melted through their clothes into a chair or mattress or the floor where they died.

But here it was in the fresh air and even the rain pounding down into the pavements and the chilly wind cutting between the buildings couldn't clear it.

And when I finally turned the corner onto the front of Victoria Station I discovered why.

In the few days I'd been at home with Dominique and Louisa, the death toll had mounted alarmingly, and for some reason Victoria Station had been chosen as a central clearing area for bodies whilst there'd still been healthy people to collect them.

Whose bloody idea that had been I couldn't guess.

The forecourt, where once taxis had plied their trade and buses had started and ended their journeys was full of trucks of all descriptions that had been used to transport the bodies. Garbage trucks, three tonners and artics were jammed up tight together. All were silent with their engines switched off, or if they'd been left running had run out of fuel. Inside many of them the drivers had been overcome by the plague and died at their posts. It was one of the most frightening sights I'd ever seen.

I passed through the ranks of vehicles and into the station and there it was even worse. I imagine the plan was to put the bodies into trains and run them out of the city. But obviously that idea had gone the way of a lot of bright ideas lately. There were bodies everywhere on the concourse, piled high against every vertical surface. It was a nightmare made flesh. Flesh that was now bloated and corrupt and leaked bodily fluids that made the floor under my feet stick to the soles of my shoes. It seemed that the bodies of people who died from The Death, and that appeared to be everyone who caught it, went bad very quickly. Nice thought.

As I stood there, seemingly the only live person in the place I heard a shout from behind me and a number of men, faces masked appeared from the door of a darkened coffee shop.

Why these ghouls had gathered there I didn't know.

Then I realised why. One of the men at the back of the group was pushing a wheelbarrow that was piled with watches, wallets, jewellery, anything of value that they could loot from the bodies. These men were robbing the dead, and they obviously thought that I was trying to muscle in on their territory.

Silently they came towards me, the leader holding a baseball bat.

That was just what I needed. The end of the civilised world, my wife, daughter, job and home gone. And now a bunch of grave robbers wanted to rearrange my body and add it to the death toll.

No chance.

I took out one of the Glocks and held it in plain sight.

But of course I should've realised that they would not only be armed with clubs. From various hiding places about their persons the men produced a frightening array of firearms and I turned and fled.

But they weren't going to leave it at that. As I charged across the concourse, splashing though the stinking effluence on the floor, bullets tore past me and ricocheted off the walls and smacked into the piles of cadavers.

I turned and fired back, wasting a couple of precious bullets, that even then, I knew would be worth their weight in gold before long.

I slipped and skidded around a pile of bodies and ran through one of the ticket barriers and down a long platform towards the cutting that entered a tunnel fifty yards or so away and headed down to the river and beyond, and on both sides of me piles of bodies covered the silver rails that led to freedom.

It was like the pit of Hades.

There was only one way out and I knew I had to take it. I looked down into the burial pit and the smell was even worse. Bodies were piled together like discarded dolls in all states of dress and undress as if some giant child had been playing with them, had grown tired of the game and emptied his toy box into a hole in the ground and left his playthings to rot.

And rot they had. With a vengeance.

The putrescence was almost visible hanging over the pit like a fine mist of decay. I went closer to the edge of the platform and my gorge rose and I vomited. I challenge anyone not under the circumstances. When it seemed like nothing was left I looked closer and vomited again. But just a thin bile forced its way up from my stomach and I spat it onto the floor. The bodies in the pit were in an advanced stage of putrescence with torsos distended, bones poking through rotten skin and it was difficult to tell what colour they had been originally as all the flesh had turned green and black as they decomposed and liquefied.

But the worst thing was the cloud of flies that fed on the bodies and the hum they made as they sated their hunger. I didn't know that flies were active at this time of year, but as it was unlike any year I'd ever lived through I was prepared to believe anything.

So I knew I had only one chance. To my right was the tunnel that led to freedom unless they too were filled with rotting bodies. My pursuers were close and getting closer and I knew that when they found me I was a dead man, so I had to take the chance of descending into the bowels of the plague pit or wait where I was and face death at their hands and be tumbled into it and rot with the rest.

I put my gun back into its holster and sat on the very edge of the platform so that my legs dangled down close to the bodies and I pushed myself off. It was only a short drop but my legs disappeared up to my knees in the liquid flesh and a huge flight of flies rose up around my head and filled my eyes, nose and mouth with their fluttering wings. But what was worse was that in the dim light that came through the filthy glass that covered that part of the station the pile of bodies seemed to move like the sea, as a million maggots rose from the depths to see what was disturbing the home that was also their food supply. I pushed the flies away from my head and tried to walk across the sea of bodies but it was like being trapped in quicksand, and with every movement of my legs I found myself sinking deeper into the corruption that surrounded me. I felt bony fingers grab at my ankles and sharper bones tore at my clothes and cut my skin, and I knew that if I could survive this without dying or going mad I could survive anything.

So with all my strength, and using any handhold I could find, I half walked, half dragged, and God forgive me, half swam towards the tunnel entrance and prayed like I've never prayed before or since that I would find some kind of escape route out of the hell I was in.

It was the most terrible few minutes of my life. Every orifice filled with slime from the bodies around me. I saw faces with the skin peeled from the skull and eyes hanging out on ganglions. I felt the flies and maggots trying to feed on me and rats started down from their tiny eyries on the brickwork as they sized me up as possible addition to their menu.

And then God, or someone, answered my prayers. Because, just as I reached the tunnel and whatever other horrors it held, I saw on the wall of the pit close by me a rotten and flaking iron ladder that led upwards into a brick chimney, just as the men who were chasing me arrived at the end of the platform. I heard their confused shouting as they searched for me in vain and I came upright, standing on piles of cadavers and grabbed for the flaking metalwork and dragged myself onto it. My clothes were in rags on my body and blood ran from a thousand cuts and mixed with the putrid flesh that coated me. I heard a shout and gunshots rang up as I pulled myself out of the green glop and hauled myself up the ladder. But someone was still looking after me. Bullets hit the brickwork and ricocheted off, some so close that I could feel the brick splinters bite into my exposed skin, but not one found its target, and within a few seconds I was safely inside the chimney and heading upwards towards the small circle of light I could see above me.

I came out into cold daylight and the rain was pouring down and I've never been so glad to see fresh air before or since.

Crying with fear and relief and disgust I tore the tattered remains of my clothes off my injured body until I stood naked except for boots, socks and my two holsters and pistols. The street I was in was deserted and a broken gutter was streaming water down onto the pavement, and I rushed towards it and stood under the freezing shower washing blood and rotting flesh off my body. How long I stood there I don't know but I couldn't seem to get clean and I haven't really felt clean since.

Afraid of being seen I ran along the street away from the train station, but I knew that every cut in my body was a possible site for infection, and I felt that I'd jumped from the frying pan into the fire. Then I saw a looted general store on the corner, its windows smashed and blind and I ran inside. There was a bloated corpse lying half on and half off the counter. God knows who he'd been, probably the owner trying to protect his property. His head was gone.

Anything wearable, drinkable or smokable was gone too, but there were still some shelves left almost untouched by the looters including the very things I was looking for. I kicked my way through the rubbish and amongst the soap powders and dusters and kitchen sponges found a dozen squeezy bottles of household bleach.

Who needed that sort of stuff at a time like this?

The answer was me.

With trembling, frozen hands I ripped the tops off the plastic bottles and covered myself in the stuff, only closing my eyes so that I wouldn't blind myself. Bottle after bottle I used, until I almost screamed with the pain as the caustic liquid found every cut and scratch on my battered body.

I only stopped when every container was empty, then I found a roll of kitchen towel and dried myself off and went into the flat at the back of the shop to try and find something to hide my nakedness.

I'll never forget that day. It's my worst horror story. Worse in a lot of ways than losing Dominique and Louisa.

Often in my dreams I return to that plague pit and the maggots and flies and rats.

But usually in my dreams I can't find a way out.

20

I WENT INTO the back of the shop which had been ransacked, and through to the bedroom where the remains of a woman was lying on the bed. She was naked, and it looked like she'd been raped before her throat had been cut, but at least whoever had done it had left her head behind. Probably she didn't have any gold teeth. I found a sweat shirt, an old jacket and a pair of sweat pants on the floor. None of them fitted particularly well but they were dry. I put them on and left through the back way.

It was still pouring with rain and I must admit I'd had better days and I was still shivering and sick to my stomach, but I kept moving.

Then I had my first bit of luck for what seemed like a year. Down a street between Victoria and Chelsea I found a small, undamaged sports and menswear shop. Behind the unbroken window on a mannequin was a waterproof jacket with a hood that looked like exactly what I needed to keep me warm and dry.

The front of the shop was barred up so I counted the numbers in the small parade, went down a service road at the side, then down its continuation at the back. There was a van parked at a crazy angle two doors away with a dead man in the driver's seat. I found a tool box in the back of the van and used a tyre iron from in it to lever open the back door of the shop and I was inside out of the rain, which had soaked me again by then.

First thing I did was to check if there was anyone alive or dead inside.

The shop was empty and it was like a goldmine in there.

It was time for us survivors to get prioritised.

Jewellery and money were no good. What we needed to keep alive was warm clothes and hot food.

And I found one and the makings of the other inside that little shop that no one had bothered to loot.

In the employee's restroom and kitchen there was coffee, tea, sugar, biscuits and sour milk inside the dead fridge, alongside a stale loaf of bread and half a packet of ham that still smelled fresh. Inside a cupboard over the sink was dried milk and two tins of vegetable soup. Water was still running from the taps.

Out front in the shop was a stock of little Calor gas stoves, enamel mugs, saucepans and plates.

I filled a saucepan with water, put it on top of the stove and lit the gas with a waterproof match from a supply behind the counter. Soon the water was boiling and I made coffee with dried milk and ate half the biscuits. I was suddenly starving.

When the worst of my hunger was assuaged and the hot drink was warming my insides I explored further.

I found the manager's office and went through the drawers of his desk. In the middle one was a packet of Silk Cut and when I shook it, it was half full.

I took one out, lit it and sat back in his chair with a sigh.

When it was finished I went into the washroom and ran a sink full of cold water and rinsed the bleach off myself. There was a cleanish towel on a hook and I scrubbed myself dry with it.

Then I did a stock take.

I found everything I needed for what I knew was going to be long hike out of London. For to stay was definitely suicide.

I dressed myself in thermal underpants, a T-shirt, a flannel shirt, a down waistcoat, a pair of stiff new Levi 501's, thermal socks and hiking boots. I shrugged into my shoulder holster and strapped the other holster round my waist. I checked the magazines on both Glocks. One had the full complement of seventeen bullets, the other twelve. I needed to find more 9mm ammunition and fast. I wiped the guns down with a rag and holstered them.

I found a hunting knife with one saw-edged blade in a cabinet under the counter, matched it with a sheath which I stuck inside my waist belt, picked out the best pair of binoculars with autozoom that I could find and slung them round my neck by their strap. Over that lot I pulled a leather jacket with a fleece collar.

Then I went into the camping department and picked out a large, lightweight rucksack with a metal frame which I filled with more clothes, another pair of boots, a Swiss Army Knife with all the attachments, my Calor stove and some spare containers of gas, a dozen boxes of matches, the lightest sleeping bag I could find and a long, beige duster coat which I still have.

I went back to the kitchen, ate a sandwich made with a couple of slices of the stale bread and the ham and heated up one of the cans of soup. After I'd eaten I packed all my supplies in one of the shop's plastic bags and put it on top of the rucksack and left after topping my outfit with the largest sized waterproof like the one I'd seen in the window, leaving it and the leather open so that I could get to the Glock around my waist with minimum effort. I knew I was going to be warm, walking, but it was still pissing down outside, the wind had come up and the temperature had dropped as it headed towards evening, and I also knew that travelling at night was best.

I walked through the rain until I came to a chemists which had been well and truly done over, but not for what I wanted. I took toothpaste and a toothbrush, shaving gear and foam, aspirin, a selection of foot care products, sticking plasters, scissors, filled a toilet bag with my plunder and packed it on top of everything else, and headed south. I reckoned it would be quicker and safer to get out of town that way.

And I was right.

21

AS MY MIND dwelt on those first few dreadful days after The Death rolled over us like an out of control truck, twilight had fallen and I looked at my watch. It was probably wrong, but it didn't matter. I only kept it going for one reason. But right or wrong it showed eight thirty and it was time to go. I touched Puppy with my toe and she sprang to attention. 'Come on,' I said. 'Duty calls.'

We walked through the soft air back to where we'd left the Land Rover and Ugly was snoozing behind the wheel but woke with a start and his gun in his hand as we got close. 'Relax,' I whispered. 'It's only us.'

'Anything?' he asked.

'No. Everything usable's gone.'

'Thought so. Are we going in?'

I nodded as I lit a cigarette, shielding the flame from prying eyes.

'What about her?' he indicated Puppy with a nod of his head.

'She stays. She can guard the truck.'

I opened the door of the motor and Ugly levered his huge form out, and I put a long lead on Puppy's collar so she had room to get out and do her business and she jumped up onto the seat he'd vacated, spun round and settled down. 'Good girl,' I said. 'Stay now. I'll leave the door open for you.'

She looked up at me with her doe eyes and I ruffled the fur on her neck.

We left the shotguns under some bushes and just took our pistols with us, and before we went I rescued one of the bottles of scotch we'd taken off the boy with the horse and cart the previous day and I slipped it into the pocket of my duster coat.

'What's that for?' asked Ugly.

'A peace offering. A sample. Whatever.'

He nodded. 'OK,' he said. 'Come on, let's go.'

And we walked together into the gathering gloom towards

the top of the hill and The Last Chance Saloon beyond.

When it came into sight it was lit up like a Christmas tree. Every one of those hundreds of coloured bulbs was lit and painted the shape of the building against the dark background of the wood behind it, and the perimeter fence and the front gate were illuminated by powerful white lights. After so long with nights lit only by the stars or a few candles it was almost frightening.

'Get a load of that,' said Ugly over the chug-chug of the generator and the sound of another old rock and roll song from inside the pub.

'Jesus,' I said. 'I haven't seen anything like that since Millennium night.'

We walked down the middle of the road towards the gates of the complex, our boot heels crunching, and the music got louder and louder as we went.

The gates were big, made from rough, unpainted timbers lashed together with wire and nails and there was some kind of gatehouse just inside from which, as we approached a figure emerged carrying a wicked looking Uzi machine pistol.

'Stop,' ordered the figure. 'Stay where you are.'

We did as we were told and a medium sized man materialised through the harsh light. 'Who are you?' he demanded.

I introduced myself and added. 'This is my partner Ugly.'

'You got that right,' said the man and I could feel Ugly bristle beside me. 'What do you want?'

'We heard you traded here,' I said. 'We've got stuff.'

'What kind of stuff?'

'All kinds,' I told him. 'But we deal with the organ grinder, not his monkey.' Brave words under the circumstances and the snout of that little gun that could spit its magazine of thirty bullets in just a few seconds, but I refused to be intimidated.

'Is that so,' said the man. 'Are you all there is?'

'That's right,' I said. 'But there could be someone up on the hill with the sights of a rifle right on your chest.'

'So there could,' said the man. 'But let's hope not because I reckon I could get off a few rounds as I went down.'

'We're alone,' said Ugly.

'Come on in. Slowly,' said the man, and we did as he said and passed through the entrance and he stepped into the gatehouse, his gun still on us and wound the handle on an old fashioned phone and put the receiver to his ear. 'There's people here,' he said and put the phone down.

A few seconds later two more men emerged from the door of the pub and trotted over the car park in our direction. One of them was carrying an H&K like the one we'd seen earlier and the other another Uzi. These people were well ordnanced and maybe my dream of all that ammunition was about to come true.

If we lived though the night of course.

22

THE MEN WHO ARRIVED were both large, bearded and intimidating. 'What have we here?' said the taller of the two who was wearing a fringed suede jacket and carrying the Heckler & Koch.

'We're traders,' I explained. 'I'm John. This is Ugly. And no jokes, he gets upset. A bloke called Ray we met on the road told us about you.'

'Ray,' said the tall man. 'Yeah. We know Ray.'

Not anymore I thought. 'We've got some stuff. We thought you might be interested,' I said.

'We're always interested.'

'Good. Then maybe we can do business.'

'You armed?' demanded the tall man. 'See the notice. No firearms in here.'

'What are those then?' I said indicating the weapons they carried. 'Breadsticks?'

'No firearms for visitors. Keeps everything friendly. Charlie here,' he indicated the gate guard. 'He keeps them inside his little shack. When you go you get them back. Now what you got? Guns, knives, hatchets. We're not fussy.'

I took out my pair of Glocks, the Colt .45, and the knife I'd taken from the sports shop in London, and Ugly surrendered his Webley and the Sterling automatic. I hated to give up my weapons and so did Ugly. But business is business.

'You come prepared,' said the tall man.

'We're traders,' I said. 'Sometimes we have to protect our stock. There's bad people out there.' I didn't bother to mention that we were probably the worst.

'Fair enough. But you won't object if we don't take your word for it. This being your first visit and all.'

I shrugged.

'Search 'em,' said the tall man to his companion from inside the pub who was dressed all in black leather and holding an Uzi carbine in his right hand.

The leather boy transferred the carbine to his left hand and did as he was told but missed the .38 I had hidden in my boot. An easy thing to do, but potentially fatal, but came up with the scotch I had in my pocket.

'What's that for?' he asked. A stupid question I thought, but then he didn't seem over burdened with brain cells.

'For whoever does the trading here,' I told him. 'A mark of our respect and a sample of our product.'

'I'll drink your health with it later.'

'I don't think so,' I said. 'Unless you're the boss, which I doubt. You probably couldn't open it without a map anyway.'

'You cheeky fucker,' he said and aimed the bottle at my head.

I dodged the blow, plucked the bottle out of his hand, tossed it to Ugly who caught it easily, pushed the machine pistol to one side, kicked his cowboy booted ankles out from under him, caught him as he fell, pushed the Uzi into his side and covered his finger on the trigger with mine.

'One touch and you're dead,' I said.

'And so are you,' said the tall man putting his H&K to my head as Charlie trained his Uzi on Ugly.

A Mexican stand-off I believe it's called.

'So why don't we all be friends and you take me to whoever runs this place?' I asked pleasantly, looking up at the tall man. 'There's no need for aggro. We come in peace, recommended by a friend of yours. You trade, we trade. We can be of mutual benefit to one another. Now what do you say?'

'You've got some bottle,' he said and I knew then that he wouldn't shoot.

'Bottle is right,' I said. 'Three cases of the best scotch to be precise. And a lot more besides. Now can I let go of this trigger? I'm beginning to get cramp in my finger, and if I do it might go off. Which won't be conducive to your friend here's health.'

There was a moment of dreadful silence only punctuated by the Rolling Stones pumping out *Exile On Main Street* from the bar, then the tall man grinned, eased his finger off the trigger of the H&K. 'OK,' he said. 'You'd better come and meet Marco.'

23

I GINGERLY UNTANGLED myself from the leather boy and his gun and offered him my hand to pull him up off the ground but he brushed it aside. Petulant, I thought.

'Next time,' he said.

'It'll be my pleasure,' I replied as I took the bottle of scotch off Ugly and put it back in my pocket.

'This way,' said the tall man. 'I'm Laurie by the way, he's Sid,' indicating the leather boy. 'And Charlie you know.'

All very polite, but I knew we'd come close to being blown away, but then it wasn't the first time. And definitely not the last.

Laurie led us across the tarmac past the line of bikes and cars to the pub leaving Sid and Charlie to talk about us when we were gone.

'You've not made a friend there,' said Laurie as we went.

'You mean he won't come to our birthday party,' grunted Ugly.

'It speaks,' said Laurie, but softened the words with a grin showing dirty teeth.

'It kicks arse too,' said Ugly so only I could hear and I grinned at him too.

The three of us went up a couple of stone steps and Laurie pushed through the double doors and for the first time we entered The Last Chance Saloon, though personally I felt as if we'd been drinking in it for months.

The inside was huge, dimly lit, hot and fairly crowded, and Laurie stopped just inside the doors so we could drink in the ambience.

I imagine that when the pub was originally built it had consisted of a number of bars, but in the style of the few years before The Death, the design consultants had been called in and had knocked the whole place through into one.

The bar itself ran most of the length of the far wall, leaving only room for two doors to its left, one marked LADIES, the other GENTS, the words having been crossed out and BITCHES and STUDS substituted in thick felt tip pen. Such decorum.

On the other side was a single door marked PRIVATE, and underneath had been added WALK IN AT YOUR PERIL.

The bar itself was long, made out of a single piece of blond wood now scarred with burns and cut with initials and messages. Behind it were the pumps and optics and a huge mirror that was cracked and crazed and peppered with bullet holes.

Two young women in cut-off T-shirts and jean shorts cut high tended the bar.

The room was carpeted, but the carpet was as distressed as the mirror behind the bar, stained and burnt and ragged. In one corner of the room beneath a DJ's console the carpet had been cut and ripped up to reveal the floorboards and make a crude dance floor. Hanging from the high ceiling above the floorboards were two huge cages made of black iron with plywood floors. To our right was a set of stairs that went up to a gallery that ran right round the bar. It was dark up there, darker than in the bar itself but I saw that a number of closed doors ran off the gallery. To our left was a serving hatch that led into the kitchen where I could see a another couple of young girls slaving over a massive industrial sized stove. Next to the hatch was a beautiful Wurlitzer bubble juke box pumping out the music we'd heard earlier.

So far, so normal. But one thing wasn't normal. Not normal at all. All around the wall stakes had been hammered into the plaster. And on the end of those stakes were human heads. Real ones I swear. In various stages of decay, from dried up husks to one that was still dripping bodily fluid. My blood ran cold at the sight and I nudged Ugly. He'd seem them too. 'Nice,' he said. 'Wonder what they did wrong.'

I wondered too, but said nothing.

At ground level the rest of the room was crammed with mismatched chairs and tables where the clientele sat.

And what a clientele.

Ladies and gentlemen one and all.

The bikers were in one corner surfing on beer and marijuana. Christ knows where they got that. The gang was made up of both men and women dressed in filthy denim and leather with lots of tattoos and body studs.

But they looked like little angels compared to some of the other citizens sprawled across the furniture.

Jesus, it was like one of those comic book versions of the end of the world. Like by the geezer who did those Batman graphic novels in the eighties. And he'd been right in his vision of the apocalypse. There were dustbowl cowboys, goths, punks, new romantics, grunge kings and queens, junkie scarecrows, bodybuilding freaks, the full nine yards. And if I'd still been a copper I'd've busted them all in a second.

That was when I saw the wisdom of confiscating weapons at the gate.

I looked at Ugly and said 'We'll be right at home here.'

'When's the wet T-shirt competition start?' was all he said in reply.

'Soon,' said Laurie. 'I see you're a man after my own heart. I'll get you a drink and fetch Marco.'

We trooped through the tables under the scrutiny of those already in and Laurie said. 'What'll you have?'

'What've you got?' I asked.

'Everything. Sufficient of everything. Stick around and you'll find out.'

'Got any cold beer?' I said.

'Draught or bottled?'

I thought he was taking the piss. 'A pint of lager?'

'Sure.'

'Two,' said Ugly. 'And make it freezing. I'm sick of drinking warm beer.'

'Janice,' said Laurie to one of the girls behind the bar who I noticed had a faded black eye. 'Two pints of lager for these gentlemen.'

'In thin glasses,' I said with a smile as a way of breaking the ice, but didn't get a smile in return.

She went to the pump and pulled two perfect pints. Ugly and I gingerly sipped at them and they were cold as ice.

'We make our own,' explained Laurie. 'There's a brewery downstairs. Enjoy. I'll go and see if Marco is free.'

He left us to it and Ugly and I turned and leant back against the bar and I lit a cigarette and turned to my friend and said. 'I know we've only been a here for a little while, but I hate this place already.'

24

AND I DIDN'T LIKE IT any the better when Marco eventually arrived a couple of minutes later.

He appeared with Laurie through the door marked PRIVATE that our tall friend had entered after he'd seen us alright with our drinks, and I thought I'd seen some bizarre sights that evening until he showed his misshapen little head, but this one took the biscuit.

He was a dwarf. Or as we would've said, in those dear dead politically correct days before The Death made fools of us all, vertically challenged.

But let's face it. The little cunt was a dwarf. About three foot six with a head like a melon someone had taken a dislike to and kicked around the room for an hour or so.

And the face on it. Man. I've seen some sights in my time, but that boat race made me want to lie down in a darkened room for an hour or so with a bottle of aspirin. His mouth was a wet little horror that most people would've disowned if they'd had it as an arsehole, his nose would've looked ugly on a pig, his eyes were lidless and the colour of dirty dishwater with no lashes or eyebrows, and his ears stuck out a pair of jug handles from a completely bald head whose skin was mottled and peeling. Christ, he made Ugly look like Steve McQueen.

He was dressed in a cute little Sergeant Pepper satin soldier suit with a pair of pearl handled Colt revolvers strapped round his waist, and at the end of a leash he held in his left hand was a black panther. An honest to God wild animal, and I wondered what zoo he'd plundered that from. I was amazed that when he walked in with Laurie close behind that the entire room didn't crack up at the sight of him.

But it didn't. Conversations did stop. But not out of disbelief at his appearance, but in deference as you'd imagine it would be like if Napoleon stopped by on the way to Waterloo for a natter.

I looked at Ugly and Ugly looked at me and we both looked at Laurie who stared back as if daring us to laugh.

'Good evening gentlemen,' said Marco in a piping little voice that still managed to cut through the sound of Creedence Clearwater Revival on the Wurlitzer. 'I hope everything is to your satisfaction. My name is Marco. Welcome to my world.'

'Pleased to meet you,' I said after a second's silence and offered him my hand.

He took it and it was a bit like holding a pilchard in olive oil fresh out of its tin. All cold and slimy and good only for feeding to a cat.

I repressed a shudder as I took it, but I knew that Marco understood and that at that instant I had made an enemy.

'You must be John,' he said. 'And your friend is Ugly.'

But not half as ugly as you I thought. 'That's correct,' I said, letting go of his fingers and resisting the urge to wipe my fingers on my coat.

'And I believe you are traders.'

'We do our bit. In fact I brought you this.' And I produced the bottle of scotch from my pocket. 'A gift,' I said. 'And a sample of some of our stock.'

'Too kind,' said Marco. 'We are always looking for new sources of supply.'

'Good,' I said. 'This is some place you have here.'

'I'm flattered you approve. But you came on foot. Surely you have transport.'

'A truck. We left it parked. We weren't sure of our welcome.'

Marco smiled. A glimpse into hell. 'You don't trust us.'

'We were simply being careful. One never knows these days.'

'Of course,' he said and one of the revolvers appeared in his hand as if by magic, and the sound of the gun cocking cut through the conversations that had resumed and the room fell silent again. Even the juke box was quiet. 'But if you came as friends you'll be treated like friends. Of course if the opposite was true I could kill you both now and I'm sure it wouldn't take long for my men to find where your truck is parked.'

'Without a doubt,' I said, looking down the muzzle of his gun which loomed as large as a tube train tunnel. 'But why bother? We could build a good business relationship. Mutually profitable.'

What I didn't tell him was that if he did kill us and found the truck, he'd also find the couple of pounds of plastique that Ugly had packed into the chassis of the Land Rover and which would detonate precisely twenty-four hours after the car was started unless certain precautions were taken. Explosives and booby traps were another of Ugly's specialities. We always figured that if the car was taken, if we didn't get it back within that time it was gone forever. That was why I still wore a watch. Just so's I'd know when twenty-four hours had gone, and the Land Rover with it.

Welcome to the modern world.

25

'**BUT WHY BE INHOSPITABLE,' SAID** Marco, and the gun vanished as swiftly as it had appeared, and I for one breathed a sigh of relief, although Ugly seemed totally unfazed by the whole incident. But then the gun had been pointing at me and not at him, which I suppose, had something to do with it. 'It's party time,' Marco went on. 'It's always party time at The Last Chance Saloon. So let's all have fun.'

'I'm up for that,' I said, and my voice sounded almost normal in my ears.

'But first,' said Marco. 'Come into the office and let's talk for a moment in private.'

'Fine by me,' I said. 'Ugly…'

'Just you John,' the little man interrupted. 'I believe your confederate is interested in the wet T-shirt competition. It's due to start in a few minutes and we wouldn't want him to miss it would we?'

'Not under any circumstances,' I said.

'So let's leave him to it.'

'Ugly,' I said again, and he just nodded and went back to his beer.

'After you,' I said and Marco and his pet led me through the door marked PRIVATE into his inner sanctum with Laurie trailing behind us, the H&K still in his arms.

'I hope that's not literal,' I said when we were inside a large office with another door leading off it to one side.

'What?' asked Marco with a look of puzzlement as he took a seat behind a large desk which had been mounted on a riser to give him some height, and the panther settled down at his feet and promptly fell asleep.

'The bit on the door about peril.'

'Forget it,' he said with a wave of one tiny paw. 'A private joke. Sit. A drink?'

'Brandy?' I ventured.

'Of course. Laurie.'

I took one of the chairs on the opposite side of the desk and Laurie leant his gun against the wall and poured me a large one in a massive balloon glass from a well stocked bar on the wall behind Marco's desk and brought it over.

'Thank you,' I said, and he nodded and retrieved his weapon and leant himself against the wall instead.

'Tell me something,' I said.

'What?'

'Those heads stuck up round the bar. Are they a private joke too?'

'Business competitors,' he replied. 'But we're not in competition are we?'

'Not at all,' I said.

'Now tell me some things,' said Marco fishing a thin cheroot from a box in front of me and offering me the same.

'I'll stick to cigarettes,' I replied, taking my packet of B&H from my pocket and lighting one. 'While they last.'

'That's the problem isn't it,' said Marco. 'How long things will last.'

'You seem to have it pretty well sussed out from what I've seen.'

'The Death was the best thing that ever happened to me,' he said with a another smile from his preposterous mouth, and I wondered how shit like this had survived whilst my family died, but I just smiled back. 'Before, I was nothing,' he continued. 'A little man in a world of giants. But now I am the giant.'

'What did you do?' I asked. Not that I really cared, but it was warm and comfortable in the room, the brandy was the best I'd tasted for months, and I had nothing else to do.

'I was an accountant. A number cruncher. A drone. And yourself?'

'I was a policeman.'

He clapped his hands and laughed out loud. 'Splendid. That's how you managed to handle Sidney.'

I looked at Laurie. He'd obviously been telling tales out of school. 'I had some training,' I admitted.

'It nearly had you and your friend killed.'

'Sid wanted to take your gift. He showed you disrespect. I simply taught him a lesson.'

Marco looked at Laurie who nodded.

'He will be punished for that,' he said. 'You and your friend make a formidable team.'

'We get along.'

'He is a man of few words.'

'He's good with his hands.'

'Of course. You need people like that. We all do. And you have a base?'

I nodded.

'Where exactly?'

'On the south coast.' I didn't elaborate, and his eyes narrowed, but he didn't push it.

'And you scavenge.'

'You could put it like that.'

'Forgive me, I don't wish to belittle what you do. We all scavenge to a greater or lesser extent these days. Tell me what you have?'

'At the moment some liquor, a little petrol, canned food. The usual. But we're nothing like as organised as you.'

'Very few are. We do well. Petrol we have plenty of. But food and booze is always needed. And coffee. Fresh coffee, vacuum packed. That would be at a premium.'

'But that would mean going into towns,' I said. 'Towns are still dangerous places. Disease. Snipers.'

'That is why we would pay a premium. What is it you need most? What would tempt you?'

'Fuel. Though we've been lucky with that. And ammunition. Ammunition mostly.'

He leant forward, put his little hands together in a steeple on the desk in front of him and the panther wriggled in its sleep at his movement. 'Now that's where I think we could help you John.'

'You do seem to have a good supply of ordnance. I'm envious.'

'We were lucky there. There was an American base close by. Come see.' And he hopped down from his perch, walked to the other door that led out of the office, opened it, and beckoned me to follow him.

Inside was an armoury. The very thing I'd been dreaming of since The Death came. There were racks of automatic rifles, crates of hand guns and a pile of ammunition as tall as me stacked in one corner. In the other were ammunition boxes, instruction manuals and bits and pieces of uniforms scattered everywhere. On the far wall was a bench, upon which were what I recognised as hand loading equipment, empty cartridge cases and boxes of gun powder.

Despite myself I whistled in admiration. 'We came across a couple of bases ourselves but they'd been stripped clean,' I said. I didn't tell him that that was where we'd found the plastique and the detonators. He might still try to steal our truck and I didn't want to spoil the surprise.

'The Yanks mostly got out early,' said Marco. 'Typical really. But we found one base that was still active. A skeleton crew were packing up when we arrived. They didn't make it.'

I was hardly listening as I examined the booty. There must've been a hundred thousand rounds of both .45 and 9mm ammunition. It was beautiful.

'And this is for sale.'

'Everything's for sale. At a price.'

'And petrol,' I said. 'I saw the tankers.'

'My motorcycle boys are good with their hands too. They can operate petrol pumps without the benefit of electricity. Pull up the fuel by hand.'

'Yeah,' I said, 'Ugly can do that too. But most garages were out of petrol long before the end. When everybody was trying to get somewhere safe.'

Marco nodded. 'True. But our coup was that one of the bike boys was an engineer at a petrol refinery in Essex. Millions of gallons, just there for the taking. We run convoys once a week. It's dirty and dangerous job but they get well rewarded.'

'Amazing.'

He was warming to his tale. 'And we have a brewery below.'

'Laurie told me,' I said.

'And a granary and mill for our bakery and there are plenty of animals ready for butchering. We have a farm close by. Fresh milk, butter, cheese.'

'Everything you need.'

'We survive. And when civilisation returns as it will. As it must. We will be ready.'

'Ready?' I queried.

'To rule,' he said. 'To rule the world.'

26

I'VE GOT TO TELL YOU, when he said it I felt sorry for the world. Or what was left of it, if this pocket-sized megalomaniac got hold of it. But all I said was, 'Well someone's got to do it.'

'Precisely. Now to more immediate matters. You're after fuel and ammunition, right?'

I nodded.

'Do you want to bring your goods in now?'

I looked at my watch. It was getting late. 'No. Tomorrow morning will do. We're in no hurry.'

'Do you wish to spend the night here? There are rooms upstairs.'

'I think we're more used to sleeping under the stars,' I replied. The thought of a night under his roof did nothing for me. We'd probably wake up in the morning with our throats cut.

'As you wish. Now I have things to do. Why don't you rejoin your friend and relax?'

'Sounds like a good idea.'

'Do it then,' and he dismissed me with a wave of his hand.

Laurie accompanied me back into the office still carrying his weapon. 'Do you sleep with that?' I asked.

'Seems like it sometimes.'

I made for the door to the bar. 'Coming?' I asked.

He nodded and I opened the door and was almost overwhelmed by the noise.

Inside, the evening's entertainment was well under way. The jukebox was silent and a young dreadlocked male had taken over the DJ console where he was spinning a couple of chunks of twelve-inch vinyl, scratching and mixing as he went. Inside the two cages a pair of go-go dancers were gyrating to the beat and on the stage half a dozen or so nubile young women wearing T-shirts and shorts had been doused with water to allow their breasts to show through the almost transparent material.

The music was at almost deafening volume and the audience were screaming their approval.

Ugly was standing at the bar with a fresh pint in front of him. I joined him and he gestured for another. 'Having fun?' I yelled into his ear.

He grinned wolfishly in reply. Not exactly subtle was Ugly.

When my drink arrived and the girl had given Laurie a scotch I lit a cigarette and looked round. It was bloody mayhem. Then I glanced at the girls on stage. I wasn't that interested to tell you the truth. That was something that had died inside me the day I lost my family. They were shuffling around the stage looking far from happy at their predicament, and one who had been at the back and I hadn't noticed at first stepped into the spotlight.

My eyes passed across her then I did a double take and before I knew what I was doing I shouted. 'Dom.' Ugly heard and gave me a strange look.

I shut my mouth and felt myself redden with embarrassment. Of course it couldn't be. Dominique was dead and buried in south London next to our daughter and my friend. But it was so much like her. Or at least so much like her when I'd first seen her more than ten years before that I couldn't keep my eyes off her.

I turned round to Laurie and grabbed his arm hard. 'Who's that girl?' I demanded, yelling into his ear.

He looked bewildered. 'Which girl?'

'On stage. The dark-haired one on the right hand side.'

He shrugged. 'Christ knows. Just a whore. The cabaret. Marco collects them.'

'I want to talk to her.'

'Why?'

'I just do.'

He leered at me. 'Just talk eh?'

I fixed him with a glare and squeezed his arm tighter. 'Just talk.'

'Alright, alright. There's rooms upstairs like Marco said. But it'll cost you.'

'Whatever it takes.'

Come on then.'

He set off across the room and I followed. He marched up to the stage and grabbed the girl by the arm and tugged her down.

She protested and I wanted to hit him but I restrained myself.

Almost ignored by the crowd as if this was a regular occurrence he pulled her between the tables and up the stairs. I followed.

At the top he threw open the second door we came to and shoved her inside. 'Have fun,' he said to me. 'Don't do anything I wouldn't.'

27

INSIDE THE ROOM was dimly lit by one small lamp on top of a table by the curtained window. I shut the door after us in Laurie's face and pushed home a brass bolt to lock it. It was furnished like some kind of vagrant's hostel with a three quarter sized bed covered in a stained quilt, an armchair with one leg propped up by an old phone book, the table and lamp and an ashtray next to it, and that was it. There was a small, grubby sink in one corner under a cracked mirror. On top of the sink was a towel. All the comforts of home, but I doubted if Marco's clientele noticed.

The girl stood on the dusty carpet and covered her breasts, which still showed through the wet cotton, with her arms. She looked terrified.

I went to the sink, picked up the towel and handed it to her. 'Dry yourself,' I said.

She turned her back, stripped off her T-shirt and did as I said. Her modesty was wasted as I could see her front in the mirror but she didn't notice.

God. She was so much like Dominique it made my insides hurt.

When she'd finished, she turned to me clutching the towel to her chest. I took off my duster coat and put it round her shoulders. She grabbed it to herself. I rescued the ashtray, sat on the armchair, took out a cigarette and offered her the packet. She shook her head.

'Sit down,' I said.

She looked at the bed and shook her head.

'You want this chair?'

Another head shake.

'Please yourself.'

'You won't hurt me will you,' she said.

'No. I won't hurt you.'

'What do you want?'

'I don't know really. To talk. What's your name?'

'Loretta.'

'Pretty name. I'm John.' I stood and put out my hand for her to shake. She looked at it as one might a scorpion.

I shrugged and sat down again.

'Why me?' she asked after a moment.

'It doesn't matter. It was a mistake.'

'Don't you want to fuck me?'

I laughed out loud. 'No.'

'Why not? Are you gay?'

I laughed again. She was funny. I hadn't laughed like that for... Who knows how long? I liked her. 'No. I'm not gay.'

She seemed to relax then and leant her bottom against the table. 'I'll have that cigarette now please.'

I took her the packet and she put her arms into the sleeves of my coat and buttoned it up. It was far too big and I helped her roll up the sleeves, something I'd often done for Louisa when she tried on adult clothes. She smelled fresh and clean. It had been too long since I'd smelt a woman too. She allowed me to help and took a cigarette and I lit it for her.

'Where do you come from?' I asked.

'Originally? Nottingham. I was working in Cambridge when The Death came.'

'Doing what?'

'Waitressing. I was waiting to go to university.'

'Cambridge University?'

'Don't sound so surprised. I'm not stupid.'

'I didn't think you were. Sorry. How old are you?'

'Eighteen.'

'Christ.'

'Why don't you do what all the other men do?'

'What's that?'

'Paw me. Hurt me.' she started to cry.

'That's not my style.' I got up and picked up the towel from where she'd dropped it on the bed and gave it to her. She mopped her eyes with one corner.

'I'd kill myself if I wasn't...'

'What?' I asked.

'Nothing.'

'Tell me.'

'I'm pregnant,' she blurted after a moment.

It was a shock. I hadn't thought about anyone being pregnant. Not since The Death. 'How long?' I asked. 'You don't look pregnant.'

'Just a couple of months. I haven't told anyone.'

'Why tell me.'

'You're kind.'

'I'm not. I've done some cruel things lately.' I'd never vocalised that before.

'Everyone has I expect. Since The Death. But down inside I know you're not like that.'

'Thank you.'

'Do you think it'll live?'

'What?'

'My baby.'

'Sorry. I don't know. Where's the father?'

'He's dead.'

'From The Death.'

'No. Marco had him killed. He did something wrong.'

'Does Marco know?'

'No. He'd do something terrible. Don't tell him.'

'I won't. So you were both immune?'

'Who?'

'You and the father.'

'That's right.'

'So the baby probably will be.'

'Not necessarily. The Death could still be around. A baby would be so vulnerable to infection.'

'There's only one way to find out.'

'I know. But I'm scared that Marco will make me abort it when I start to show. God, I hate this place.'

'It wouldn't be my first choice for a holiday I agree. How

come you're here?'

'Marco finds people. He found me. I was hungry and frightened. There were so many terrible things happening when the The Death came.'

'I know. I saw some of them.'

'At least here we get to eat regularly.'

'But not without giving something in return. Right?'

'Marco wants our souls.'

'So leave.'

'I can't. No one leaves without Marco's permission.'

'I do.'

'Have you tried?'

'No.'

She pulled a wry face and stubbed out her cigarette in the ashtray.

'Nobody keeps me where I don't want to stay,' I said. 'And as for Ugly...'

'Who's Ugly?'

'My partner in crime.'

'That big man by the bar.'

I nodded.

'He scared me.'

'Don't worry about Ugly. He wouldn't hurt you.'

'I think I've heard that somewhere before.'

'It's true. I would never lie to you.' Now why did I say that? It was because of her resemblance to Dominique. Or maybe it was what was inside her belly. A new life. A miracle. Maybe a new start for us all. It took me less than a second to make the decision. 'You can come with us if you like,' I said.

'We'd never get through the front door. I'm Marco's property and he'd never let me go.'

I held out my hand. 'Wanna bet?'

28

THE RACKET was just as loud outside as we left the room and I led the way down the stairs, Loretta picking up the skirts of my coat so as she didn't fall. Ugly was still where I'd left him at the bar, but there was no sign of Laurie.

We weaved our way through the crowd back to him and I shouted. 'Where's the other fella?'

'He went back in there.' And he gestured to the office door.

'We're leaving,' I said.

'Yeah.'

'Yeah. And she's coming with us.'

'How did I guess? I don't think the little bloke's going to be too pleased.'

'Fuck his luck.'

Ugly smiled a big grin and I said. 'Ugly meet Loretta. Loretta, Ugly.'

Loretta smiled shyly and Ugly said. 'Pleased to meetcha.'

'Come on then,' I yelled above the din. 'We'd better make our farewells.'

'Why don't we just go,' Ugly shouted back.

'That'd never happen. And he's got some stuff we need.'

I went to the door marked PRIVATE with Loretta and Ugly close behind and hammered on it with the side of my fist. After a moment Laurie opened it. 'I want to see Marco,' I said.

I heard the little man shout 'Who is it?' from inside.

Laurie turned and said 'The new bloke.'

'Let him in.'

Laurie pulled the door fully open and we all went inside.

'Well well,' said Marco when the door was closed behind us to keep out the noise. 'I see you've made a new friend already.'

I nodded. 'We're leaving,' I said. 'And she's coming with us.'

Marco clapped his hands and laughed. 'I don't think so,' he said.

'I'll pay,' I said. 'Anything you want.'

'She's not for sale.'

'I thought you said that everything was for sale,' I rejoindered.

'Not her.'

'Then I'll just take her.'

'Why?'

'That doesn't matter.'

'You must be a very arrogant man to think you can just walk in and take whatever or whoever you want away with you.'

'Maybe.'

'Or very foolish.'

'Maybe that too. But whatever. She comes with us. Now.'

Marco got up from his seat and stood in front of me on the edge of the riser. Even then, his head hardly came up to my shoulder. 'I still can't understand why you want to take her,' he said. 'She's just a piece of trash.'

'Because she wants to leave. That's why.'

'Then I'm afraid you're both going to be very disappointed.'

'I don't think so,' I said and I reached down and took the .38 from inside my boot, and cocking the hammer as I brought it out, I stuck it into Marco's face. 'Your men missed this. Ugly get those pop guns he's wearing.' Out of the corner of my eye I saw Laurie begin to bring his gun up. 'Laurie. Don't even think about it,' I said. 'This is a hair trigger. I go. He goes with me.'

Ugly pulled the twin .45's from Marco's holsters, dropped one into his pocket and cocked the other and pointed it at Laurie.

'Gimme,' I said to him.

'What?'

'The H&K,' I said. 'Now.' He passed it to me and I turned it and slammed the butt into his face so that his nose broke with an audible pop and he dropped to the ground. I casually kicked him in the ribs but he didn't move. 'That'll teach you to take the piss out of my mate,' I said.

Marco looked amazed at the speed that things had happened. 'You won't get away with this,' he protested.

'I think we will. Now in the other room. You've got some things there we need.' For the first time Marco looked alarmed.

I hooked the H&K over my shoulder on its strap and kept the .38 close to his skull. 'Come on, quick,' I said. 'We haven't got all day.'

He preceded us into the room and Ugly's eyes widened at what he saw. 'Christ,' he said. 'It's Christmas.'

'Get one of those ammunition boxes and fill it with bullets,' I ordered. 'Nine mills and forty-fives. I'll keep an eye on laughing boy here.'

Ugly did as he was told. 'Loretta,' I said. 'See if any of those clothes fit. You need something to wear.'

She picked up a sweater from the floor and held it against herself, pulled a face, slipped off my duster and pulled it over her naked breasts. Ugly stopped what he was doing. 'Get on with it,' I said. 'It's not a show.'

She found some uniform pants and pulled them over her shorts.

'That's better,' I said. 'Now get that bag.'

On the floor was an old Nike sports bag. She picked it up. 'What's this for?' she asked.

'The guns in the gatehouse. I want them all.'

'You'll never get that far,' spat Marco.

'I think we will,' I said, putting my coat back on being careful not to take the barrel of the .38 out of Marco's face as I did it.

'You won't even get through the bar.'

'We will with you with us,' I told him.

Meanwhile Ugly had finished packing ammunition into the box and hefted it. 'Bloody heavy,' he said.

'We'll manage. Right. You go first with our friend here. You next Loretta, and I'll bring up the rear with the box. And be careful. If it all goes off we're in deep shit.'

Marco sneered and I smacked him round the face with my free hand. 'Just keep it buttoned, you,' I warned.

So that's how we went. Ugly picked up Marco like he was a feather and screwed the barrel of one of his own .45's into his ear with the hammer cocked. Loretta followed close behind him carrying the sports bag, and I hefted the weight of the ammunition box onto my shoulder by its khaki strap, dropped my .38 into my pocket, checked that the H&K was ready to fire and followed them.

'Hey Ugly,' I said as he put his hand on the handle of the door into the bar.

'What?'

'Just in case. It's been nice knowing you.'

'Cheers,' he said dryly.

29

UGLY OPENED THE DOOR gently and we filed through, him at the front carrying Marco in his left arm with his massive hand over his mouth, and in his right fist one of Marco's pistols with the barrel stuck into the soft part of his neck, Loretta close behind him carrying the sports bag and me at the back with the ammo box over one shoulder and the H&K ready to rock in my hands.

We kept close to the wall and for the first ten yards or so no one noticed that we were there.

Then the DJ who was facing us saw what was happening and the music suddenly stopped as he pushed the arm of the deck across the record with a terrible screeching sound.

People saw where he was looking with a stunned expression and they turned as one in our direction as the dancing girls stopped in mid boogaloo. Suddenly all eyes were on us and there was a deadly silence in the bar.

I worked the mechanism of the machine pistol and it rang out loud above the silence. 'Keep going,' I said to Ugly and Loretta and then to the crowd. 'We're leaving now brothers and sisters and if anyone tries to stop us, they're dead, then Little Caesar gets it too.'

We picked up speed and I swivelled the barrel of the H&K around. I knew there were supposed to be no firearms in the room, but if I'd got my .38 in without any trouble, Christ knows what other ordnance was stashed away in there.

Ugly hit the front door, Loretta followed and I stood in the doorway and said. 'Give us a minute and he'll be OK. Follow us and he dies.' And with that I let the door swing shut behind me and I turned to see what delights waited for us outside.

Charlie and Sid were nowhere to be seen and Ugly and Loretta were running across the car park towards the gate. I followed, running backwards keeping the door covered.

I came to the line of bikes all neatly parked in a row and I had an idea. I screwed the petrol cap off the first one and gave it a hefty kick, and like a row of dominoes, one by one they tumbled over, petrol from the first one's tank splashing everywhere.

At the sound of the bikes falling I heard a shout from behind and turning, saw Sid standing by the gate with Ugly now pointing the pistol into his face.

'Get down on the ground and lose the weapon,' roared Ugly and Sid dropped to a prone position and Loretta rescued his gun.

Then Charlie got into the act. He came charging out of the gatehouse and Ugly dropped him with a single bullet.

'Get the guns,' I screamed at Loretta and she vanished inside the gatehouse as the door to the bar opened, several figures were silhouetted against the light inside and I heard shots, saw the muzzle flashes and bullets whipped past me. I pulled the trigger of the H&K and it jumped in my hands as the thirty shot magazine emptied in less than two seconds and the spray of bullets chopped down those stupid enough to show themselves and the bar door swung shut again.

I raced to where Ugly was still holding Marco and picked up Charlie's Uzi and switched it to full auto and sprayed the car park and the front of the pub again. A spark from one of the bullets ignited the petrol from the motor bike and with a whoosh the lot of them caught fire as Loretta dashed out of the gatehouse, the bag now heavy with weapons and I yelled, 'Get going. I'll catch you up.'

Ugly grinned and drop kicked Marco into the centre of the flames and pulled the ammo box off my shoulder, shoved Loretta out of the gate and they were gone.

I emptied the Uzi's magazine and followed them up the road, then through a gap in the hedge and across the field towards where the Land Rover was hidden.

Relieved of the weight of the ammunition I overtook the pair of them and Ugly tossed me the car keys. The driver's door was open like we'd left it and Puppy was standing on the front seat. I picked her up and threw her into the back of the truck, opened the back door on my side, jumped into the driver's seat, leant over and opened the other passenger door, operated the safety switch for the detonator of our home made bomb and stuck the key into the ignition and switched on.

The hours of tinkering that Ugly had done with the engine paid off as it started first time and purred as sweetly as a kitten.

Loretta was just a step or two behind me and she dived into the back next to Puppy who gave a surprised yelp, then Ugly was in the seat next to me, the ammo box on the floor in front of him and I put the truck into gear and set off down the lane.

'What's down here?' I yelled to Loretta as I drove without lights.

'I don't know,' she said breathlessly.

'Shit. Well we'll soon find out,' I said, and a five bar gate was in front of us which the Land Rover effortlessly demolished and we were running through a field of wheat gone to seed, then the car smashed through another gate and I pulled hard right onto a paved road and switched on the lights.

'We certainly made some friends there,' said Ugly.

'Yeah. You could say we put a dent in their day,' I added.

'Shit,' he said and started to laugh and I joined in and even Puppy seemed amused.

'What are you two laughing at?' demanded Loretta. 'That wasn't funny.'

'Oh yes it was,' I said.

'We could've been killed.'

'So what. Look around. We're doomed anyway,' I replied.

'So if we're doomed why did you bring me?' she demanded again.

Ugly looked at me and turned and I saw his face in the reflected lights from the headlamps that bounced back from the high hedges that were rushing by on both sides of us. 'Because you remind him of his wife,' he said above the roar from the engine.

I couldn't believe what he'd said. 'What?' I shouted. 'What do you mean?'

He turned back and looked at me then. 'Haven't I ever told you John,' he said. 'You talk in your sleep.'

30

'**NO**. You never told me that.' I replied. 'I'll have to be more careful in future won't I?'

He said nothing in reply and as we drove I kept glancing in his direction, wondering what it was I'd talked about in my sleep. As if I didn't know or couldn't guess.

'Where are we going?' asked Loretta when it seemed we were safe from pursuit.

'Home,' I said. 'Get all this stuff sorted.'

'Home,' echoed Ugly. 'Great. I can't wait to see the girls.'

'Where's home?' said Loretta.

'On the south coast,' I explained. 'Well out of the way.'

'And you live with women?'

'Ugly does,' I replied. 'I don't. Just Puppy.'

Puppy was sitting next to Loretta, her head on Loretta's lap and an adoring look in her eyes as Loretta played with her ears.

'How many women?' asked Loretta. Typical. Get a woman on board and all they do is ask questions.

'Just four. But a couple of them bat for the other team.'

'What?'

'Lesbians,' I said. 'Don't worry, you'll see.' And I left it at that.

In the old days before The Death, the drive from Cambridge to Lewes could have been done in an afternoon. But now, with all the obstacles we had to overcome it took a day and a half, especially as the first few hours and the last were at night. But we were in no hurry. My main concern being that no one from The Last Chance Saloon was following us. Even at a distance. I drove as slowly as was necessary, but as fast as I dared to get away. Some of the roads were clear but most were littered with blockages of one kind or another. We hadn't travelled this way before and what with all the hacking and backing up and driving cross country I was in no rush to do it again.

But we finally made it and drove along the coast road close

to the town and struck inland and found the old farm we'd taken over as our base of operations.

I steered the Land Rover up the track that wound through a small forest as dawn was breaking. It was very early and the air was chilly and fresh. There hadn't been a lot of conversation on the way. Mostly Ugly asking Loretta about herself. She wasn't that forthcoming. Before we came to the house I stopped the truck, jumped out and checked out a little box I'd built and nailed to the back of one of the trees, well out of sight of the road. Inside was a twenty-four hour-glass full of sand. It was the signal that everything was OK at the house when anyone was away. At noon precisely each day, come hell or high water we took it in turns to walk down and turn the glass over. It was simple. No mechanics, no batteries. By my calculation if everything was alright the glass should be about a quarter full at the top. It was. I turned and gave Ugly the thumbs up, then got back behind the wheel and drove the last mile.

I tooted the horn to clear a few chickens pecking at the gravel at the front of the house and braked the truck to a halt. 'Welcome to Rancho Notorious,' I said to Loretta.

As we climbed wearily out of the Land Rover, the front door opened and Pansy appeared carrying the rifle she always picked up when she heard an engine.

'Put it down Pansy,' said Ugly. 'It's only us.'

She grinned broadly, propped the gun against the doorjamb, ran down the stairs and into his arms. He picked her up, swung her round and covered her face with kisses. 'Jeez, but I've missed you,' he said.

'Me too you big lug' she said breathlessly as he let her down. Then she noticed Loretta getting out of the truck and got that sort of proprietorial look that women always do when a strange one appears on their territory. 'Who's this?' she asked suspiciously.

'That's Loretta,' replied the big man. 'Don't worry. I think she's with John.'

31

'**VERY FUNNY,**' I said to Ugly, then to Pansy. 'Where are the others?'

'Touchy,' she said with a grin, which took the sting out of the word. 'In the kitchen.'

The kitchen was at the back of the house and all four of us trooped through to where Brenda, Sandy and Gwen were sitting round the big kitchen table that dominated the room.

About the girls. Pansy was nineteen, maybe twenty. Blonde, pretty and a killer. I think she'd been raped early on after The Death came. Now she never went anywhere without a 9mm in her jeans and the Browning .30-30 lever action rifle on a sling. She was with Ugly, as was Sandy. Sandy was like our mother. Mid-forties, red hair and a flick knife. Brenda and Gwen were lesbians. Brenda was a diesel dyke who dressed in denim dungarees and could cook like a dream. Gwen was her femme. Blue denim too. But with lacy blouses. Both of them were killers too. But we were firm friends. I loved and trusted those women like I loved and trusted Ugly. It was the kind of love and trust that can only grow out of perdition. Sometime I'll tell you how we met, but not right now.

'You're back,' said Brenda and came to her feet as we entered. Ugly and I hugged her and Gwen and Sandy.

'With a surprise,' said Pansy. 'John's got a girlfriend.'

I looked at Loretta and shook my head by way of an apology. 'Ignore them,' I said. 'They don't get out much.'

'I don't mind,' she replied.

'I do. Now listen you lot. This is Loretta. We took her away from some nasty people up near Cambridge. They might be looking for her, they might not. We also took some ordnance that'll come in very useful, and I've got an idea that we might be able to get enough fuel off them to keep us warm this winter. But the main thing is that she's pregnant.'

The girls looked amazed. Like all of us I suppose it was something we hadn't thought about. I'd seen children who'd survived The Death, but only a couple of babies. They seemed to be affected worse than adults, and I didn't know if they'd survived. Certainly I'd never heard of a baby being born since the plague came. Maybe the virus or whatever it was was still floating about waiting for new victims. Maybe it had vanished as quickly as it had come. Who knew? But whatever it was the main question would be: Could a baby survive, even with two immune parents?

The girls all started talking at once but I shushed them and held up a hand for silence. 'Hold your horses' I said. 'Listen. We're all tired. We had to kill people to get Loretta away and we've been on the road ever since. I don't know about her and Ugly, but all I want is some food and to sleep. We can talk all you want later.'

Brenda smiled at me and then at Gwen. 'We've still got some real coffee left. Make a pot, there's a love and I'll rustle up some breakfast. Pansy, show Loretta to one of the spare rooms and make her up a bed. Then I'm sure you and Sandy will want to welcome Ugly home in your own way. Gwen and I'll look after the house and we'll make a welcome home dinner. We've got a lot to talk about.'

So after everyone had introduced themselves to Loretta properly, that's exactly what happened.

32

AFTER WE'D HAD BREAKFAST we all went our separate ways. Loretta to the room Pansy had prepared, me to mine, and Ugly to his with Pansy and Sandy. We wouldn't be seeing those three for a while. Puppy made it clear she wanted to be with Loretta. She'd fallen in love and there was nothing I could do about it. The fickleness of women never failed to amaze me, but I didn't bother making any comment.

But of course, after all the excitement of the last couple of days plus the unaccustomed caffeine in the coffee that Brenda had made I couldn't sleep. Instead I lay in the quiet of my room at the top of the house thinking about Marco and his gang. We'd explained to the girls about what had happened and Brenda and Gwen were sorting out the guns and ammunition we'd hijacked from them. I'd told them to separate grenades, pistols, a couple of machine guns and ammunition and stash them away in a hideyhole we'd built under an old cottage that sat a quarter of a mile away in the woods. We'd fitted it out with beds and supplies in case anything happened to the house. The rest they were to put down in the cellars beneath us where we kept our armoury. I didn't want everything together just in case Marco found us. The farm was secluded and no one but us had ever been there since we'd found it months before, with its one solitary occupant dead in his bed in a room we'd never used since. Call it superstition if you like, but after all we'd been through superstitions were returning. Religion would be next and before you knew it we'd be burning witches again. We'd carried his rotting body outside in his bedclothes and buried him on the cliff top looking out over the sea marking his grave with a simple cross. I thought it was the least we could do under the circumstances as we were appropriating his home. It was perfect for what we needed. The original building I imagined dated from the twenties, but over the years all sorts of extensions had been tagged on. There were half a dozen bedrooms not including the one where our host had died, all with en-suite bath-rooms. The living room and dining room were connected with massive oak doors that could open up into one huge area that covered half the ground floor. There was a library full of books that you might actually want to read and a fully fitted kitchen complete with wood burning stove. A further bonus was that all the reception rooms had huge working fireplaces.

We also took on the ownership of his chickens that had miraculously survived and a couple of half wild cats that lived in the barn. From what I could gather from the papers I'd found he was a writer who'd retired to the country on what he'd earned with a successful series of novels. It seemed a sad way for him to end his retirement. But then life's cruel.

As for Marco finding us, it was in the lap of the gods. We dealt with a sort of hippie commune that had come together in an old manor house just outside Lewes and a bunch of women who lived high on the beach under the cliffs in an encampment of old boats like something out of Charles Dickens. But neither camp knew exactly where we were based. Apart from them we tended to move further afield to do business. It was a case of cross our fingers and hope that our whereabouts remained a secret. We'd done some damage to Marco, but more to his pride than anything else so far.

But with what I had planned for the future it was more than his pride that would be hurt, and if he was our enemy now, he'd be our deadly enemy soon.

33

WE GATHERED TOGETHER again at six for dinner. Ugly looked smug as he sat between Sandy and Pansy. He'd obviously had a good afternoon. Loretta looked rested and less stressed out than she had been. Puppy sat with her head on Loretta's lap all through the meal, accepting the occasional scrap from her plate. Brenda and Gwen had done a great job with the cooking, incorporating some of the food we'd brought back with our existing supplies, including a chicken they'd killed especially. And there were cigarettes to smoke, beer, wine and brandy to drink. The only sad and worrying thing I could think was that, for every bottle of booze we drank, there was one less in the world. Still, someone would start brewing and fermenting again soon. It had to happen.

When we'd finished eating I called for quiet and started laying out my plan.

'Summer's going to be over soon,' I said. 'And we don't know how bad the winter's going to be. We've had some odd ones recently. Global warming gone arse upwards. We've got to expect the worst. And we're not ready for it.'

Brenda went to argue but I raised a hand to stop her.

'Just a minute Bren,' I said. 'Let me have my say, then you can pull what I'm saying to pieces if you want. Like I said we're not ready for bad weather. I know we've been laying in supplies since we came here, but look at what we just ate. We're consuming faster than we're stocking up. So something's got to be done about that and fast. There's six of us here, seven if Loretta wants to stay, and then there's the baby. I'm sure she's healthy enough to feed it herself, but we've only got so much tinned milk after that.'

I looked at Loretta. 'Do you want to stay?' I asked.

She looked me straight back. 'You've been good to me,' she said in a whisper. 'Risking your lives getting me away from Marco. Yes. If I can I'll stay. I'll help with whatever you need.'

'When's the baby due?' I asked.

'January I think.'

'So that's eight of us by the worst part of the winter.'

Nobody mentioned the chance that the baby wouldn't survive. I was glad about that.

'It's a shame so many cows died when no one was milking them at the start of all this,' I went on.

'The hippies have got a couple of cows,' said Ugly.

'You're right,' I said. 'Maybe we could do a trade for something. But that's not our immediate problem. What is, is heat and light here during the winter. We've got lots of wood to burn in the fireplaces for warmth, and in the Aga for cooking, but I don't intend to spend months living by candlelight as if it was the middle ages.'

I turned to Loretta to explain. 'One of the reasons we chose this place is because there's a working generator for the electricity,' I said. 'But we've never been able to get enough petrol for surplus. To run the lights and the central heating and the big freezers in the basement so that we could hunt fresh meat. But Marco told me about running those petrol tankers to Essex to the refinery there. What do you know about that?'

'They go about once a fortnight,' she said. 'Every tenth or eleventh day. They're gone for a couple of days at a time.'

'What's the routine?' I asked.

'What do you mean?'

'Do they both go?'

She smiled and nodded. 'Yes. Two tankers, the Range Rover and six or seven bike riders with guns.'

'Jesus,' I said. 'Quite a convoy. How many in the tankers?'

'Two men in each. And two or three in the Range Rover.'

'All armed?'

She nodded again.

I did my sums. 'So there's as many as fourteen people each trip.'

A third nod. 'So?' she asked.

I looked at Ugly. He was miles ahead of me. 'It's dangerous,' he said.

'What is?' demanded Loretta, looking back and forth between us.

'Waiting until they're full, then taking them away from Marco.' I answered.

She went white. 'You're crazy,' she said. 'He'd go insane. You don't know him.'

'Too bad,' I replied. 'Who's up for it?'

One by one everybody nodded. All except Loretta.

I looked at her hard. 'We'll need your help,' I said. 'You know the territory.'

'Marco will find out who did it and come looking for you,' she said.

'Not if we kill them all,' I replied.

There was silence around the table as our small band digested that thought.

Then Brenda lifted her glass and said. 'Kill them all and let God sort them out.'

And one by one we clinked our glasses together and repeated her deadly toast.

'Loretta?' I said.

'I still think you're crazy,' she said. But after a moment she too clinked her glass against ours and the die was cast.

34

IT GOT DARK and we lit candles and Ugly put a huge pot of water on the top of the Aga for the washing up, and we finished the brandy and watched a couple of moths dive-bombing the flames and spoke no more that night about our plans to rob Marco.

When the kitchen was tidy we bade each other good night and rather tipsily went to bed. This time Puppy deigned to come with me.

I fell straight asleep that time but came awake suddenly as the dog whined, and I reached for the pistol I always keep locked and loaded under my pillow.

The moon was full in the satin sky outside and a beam fell across the top of my bed and glinted on the bluing of the weapon as I peered around the room still half asleep and half drunk.

'Don't shoot,' said a voice I recognised as Loretta's and I saw her standing inside the doorway as she closed the door behind her with a click.

'Don't ever do that,' I said wiping the sleep from my eyes and gently lowering the hammer of the Glock. 'It could be dangerous.'

'I'm sorry,' she said. 'I couldn't sleep.'

'What do you want?' I asked as I replaced the gun and Puppy went to her and licked her hand.

'Just to talk.'

I plumped up a pillow behind my head and looked at her in the silver light from the moon. 'What about?'

'Lots of things. We haven't had a chance. Can I get into bed with you?'

I shook my head. 'No. Sit in the chair. Do you want to light a candle?'

It was her turn to shake her head. 'Please. It's cold.'

I smiled. 'There's a blanket in the chest.'

I saw her pout, but she opened the old chest in the corner and took out one of the spare blankets I kept there, tossed it round her shoulders and sat in the armchair that faced the end of the bed. 'Why did you bring me?' she asked.

'Because you were scared and pregnant and Marco didn't want to let you go.'

'A macho thing?'

'If you like. But a bit more than that I think... I hope.'

'Like what?'

'Like what I was before.'

'What were you?'

'A policeman.'

She laughed. 'Good God,' she said. 'A copper. And you were married.'

'That's right.'

'Tell me about it?'

I shook my head again. 'I don't talk about my family.'

'Dead?' she asked.

'What do you think?'

'I'm sorry.'

'Thank you.'

She changed the subject then. 'What about the others?'

'The others?' I asked.

'The girls and Ugly. How did you get together? Come to this place? Do you talk about that?'

I suddenly felt mean at my rudeness. 'Yes,' I said. 'I talk about that.'

'Then tell me.'

So I did.

35

I LIT ONE OF MY REMAINING CIGARETTES as much to give
me a chance to think as anything else, and let my mind run back to
what happened over the next few dreadful days after my trip into
what I still think of as the pit of hell at Victoria Station. I gathered
my thoughts and started. I told Loretta how I walked southwards
looking for God knows what. Just something to make me forget
the pain at losing everything. My family, my job, the world as I'd
always known it, and almost my life.

There was madness in the air then. The Death was at its height.
People were dying in the streets and left to rot. All public services had broken down. Suddenly the centre had gone. There
was no social security. No TV, no radio, no police, no government to tell the citizens what to do. We'd gone soft as a nation.
Everyone knew their rights, but few accepted the responsibili-
ties that came with them. We'd been nannied for so long that
we didn't know how to look after ourselves. But I knew. And
the more I saw of the carnage and the anarchy that had come
with The Death, the more I knew that I had to harden my heart
and be as ruthless as the disease itself. And that was why,
months later I wouldn't allow Loretta to join me in my bed,
although there was nothing I wanted more.

A lot of those that weren't dying were going insane. Literally. I saw people who I suppose had lost as much as me, running, screaming, tearing at their clothes until they were naked,
and then their skin and then their flesh. And others were hunting in packs, killing anyone else who moved. And then turning
on their own number if they coughed or sneezed or vomited
blood as The Death struck them too. Luckily most of them were
only armed with baseball bats or various other clubs and I only
had to show them one of my guns to send them looking for
weaker prey. But others had found or stolen firearms of various
kinds. But not many. I thanked God many times for our draco-
nian gun laws then because I only had so many bullets and I

didn't want to waste them. I knew even harder times were coming and that I'd need every one of them then. And I had to walk because all the streets out of the capital were clogged with cars full of the dead.

The first night I slept in a house in Brixton with a dead man in the bed upstairs. Most dwellings had dead bodies in them by then. There was no light or heat, but there were some tins of food which I warmed over my Calor gas stove in the living room with all the curtains drawn, and I slept on the sofa with a Glock in my hand and listened to the screams and moans of the dying and the curses of the living and the occasional gunshots from outside. There was water in the taps but I wouldn't drink it until it was boiled. With all the dead bodies there were around I knew there was a definite chance of cholera or something similar. I had to get out of London, and the sooner the better.

36

I LEFT THE HOUSE the next morning as the sun began to rise after a breakfast of sweet biscuits and tea. There was no sign of life as I walked up Brixton Hill towards Streatham, but I kept in the shelter of trees and buildings, never knowing where a sniper might lurk. There was a smell of burning in the air and looking back towards the city I could see palls of smoke rising behind me.

I kept on walking as the sun rose higher in the sky and the temperature rose with it and the sweet smell of decaying flesh overrode the burning. Spring had arrived and it would soon be summer and the thought of the way the millions of corpses in London would rot lent speed to my feet.

By then the crazies and hunting packs were coming out from where they'd spent their nights. I kept my hand on the Glock around my waist as I continued my journey.

I had my next confrontation as I passed Streatham Station. On the opposite side of the street was a small market and as I came to the door it burst open and three people emerged carrying bags of groceries. There were two men and a woman. The men were scruffy and unshaven and the woman was young and probably attractive, but her clothes were dirty and although she wore makeup it did not disguise the bruises on her face. They skidded to a halt at the sight of me and I could smell the miasma of liquor that hung around them.

'What have we here?' said the man at the front of the trio. 'Going camping?'

I stepped back and raised my left hand in a placatory fashion. My right I kept on the butt of my gun. I tried to smile. 'Just passing through,' I said.

'Passing through,' slurred the woman and I saw that one of her front teeth was missing, leaving a bloody gap in her gum. 'Who the fuck do you think you are?'

'Where are you heading?' said the other man. He seemed to be the most sober of the trio.

'Out of London,' I replied.

'Going to the country,' said the woman and produced a bottle of scotch from her bag and took a swig. 'Alright for some.'

'Why bother?' asked the first man. 'There's nothing in the fucking country. Just sheep.'

'Sheep,' echoed the woman. 'You a sheep shagger then?'

I smiled again although it felt forced even to me. 'No,' I replied. 'I just don't think it's going to be too pleasant here soon.'

'Pleasant,' repeated the woman again, and I knew she was going to be the troublesome one. 'Nothing's pleasant anymore mate. Have a drink.' And she offered me the bottle.

'No thanks,' I said. 'Too early for me.'

'What's in the rucksack?' the first man asked.

'Just some clothes. Nothing much,' I said back.

'Let's have a look.'

I shook my head.

'Cunt,' said the woman and aimed the bottle at me. It smashed against the wall beside my head and I took out the Glock and drilled a neat hole in her forehead. The force of the 9mm bullet at such close range blew the back of her head off and showered her companions with blood, brain and bone splinters. They stood and looked at me and I knew that I couldn't allow them to be in a position to follow me.

'Ruthie,' said the first man, looking down at the woman's body, and I pulled the trigger and knocked him to the ground with a hit in the torso.

The second man backed away and I fired again hitting him in the stomach. All three were lying on the floor, dead or soon be dead before the echoes of the shots died. My hand wasn't even shaking as I returned the pistol to its holster. My heart had hardened just as I knew it must if I was to survive. I stepped over the bodies and kept walking. The only pisser was that it was a waste of bullets.

I carried on through Norbury as the afternoon wore on and then I saw a sight I hope I never see again.

As I approached Croydon and the end of the outer suburbs

and the beginning of the countryside I saw that the whole town was in flames.

I've never been exactly fond of what the town planners did to the centre of Croydon after the war, building a haphazard collection of high rise buildings like a sort of low rent Manhattan, but to see it destroyed in one short afternoon was a strange experience.

I rested my weary feet halfway up Beaulah Hill on the back porch of a small detached house that thankfully was deserted, and drank warm beer from a can I found in the living room and looked at the flames as the sun set and the smoke drifted across the golden orb and turned it orange and purple and I realised that our civilisation had indeed ended.

37

ONCE AGAIN I rose early the next morning from my temporary accommodation of the sofa in the house in Beaulah Hill and continued my trek. I bypassed Croydon, which was still smouldering, and kept on roughly in a southerly direction. I fancied the seaside as my ultimate goal. The sea breezes would make a pleasant change from the stench of death, and I knew there were isolated houses on the downs that perhaps I could make into a permanent home.

With Croydon behind me the amount of abandoned cars became less, but it would still be impossible to drive without heavy moving machinery going in first. Anyway I was quite enjoying my walk, although it did cross my mind to find a 4x4 and head cross country. But the weather was warm and it was for sure there was no hurry. In those days there was still food easily found in houses and shops, as the vultures hadn't yet had the chance to clear them out. That would come later.

I carried on through Banstead following the road signs to Leatherhead and keeping as much as possible to what small amount of countryside still existed around what had once been small towns but were now just the outer suburbs of England's capital city. Although by then of course, the idea of a capital city or England itself was purely academic.

The further I went the more open space there was and I was glad of the kit I'd picked up at the sports shop in Victoria.

The third night I spent in another deserted house and halfway through the fourth I came across another amazing sight in a week full of them.

I'll never forget the view as I crested the hill by the M25 outside Leatherhead. The road in both directions was a jam of stalled cars that reflected the sun from paintwork and glass. It was dead quiet and I could not see a single person moving. I stopped dead and brought my binoculars up to my eyes. Their magnification showed the true state of the motorway, and as the breeze changed I caught the stink of corruption to which I'd become so accustomed. What at first had seemed to be still I could now see was alive with parasitic life. Flies hovered over the cars that had turned into coffins as the drivers and passengers succumbed to The Death, and cats, dogs, foxes, and mice and every other rodent and beast scampered in and out of the vehicles feeding on the corrupt meat within. Bodies in various stages of decomposition lay on the verges of the road. Just thinking of how many bodies there were on that stretch of road was mind boggling. And if this sort of thing was happening all over the world, and all the signs were that it was, then the whole planet was just a massive charnel house rotating round the sun. It was then that I came close to just putting the barrel of one of my guns into my mouth and finishing it all, but somehow I calmed myself down and continued my journey.

It was a river of death between me and the south and I walked along the hilltop looking for a bridge or tunnel with which to cross it.

Then I saw the first sign of human life.

As I passed through a small copse of trees I saw below a motorway service area. The car park was full and there were two people walking across it towards the buildings that made up the services themselves. Then another came through the doors and joined them. All three were armed with shotguns. At first I intended to move on further, cross the motorway and keep on going. But I was lonely for human company that wasn't mad or murderous, and even though the trio down below had guns they didn't seem intent on shooting each other out of hand and they looked quite sane. And they might have some news of what was happening in the rest of the world. I knew it was a risk, but what the hell. Everything was a risk these days.

I walked down the hill into a stronger stink of death and wondered how they managed to live in it. As I got closer to the services I unstrapped the pistol from around my waist, stashed the holster in one of the pockets of my rucksack and pushed the Glock down into my right boot.

There was a fence surrounding the services but in places it had been smashed down and I passed through and onto the tarmac.

The services area was brightly lit even in the daytime and I surmised that the power came from some kind of emergency generator. My guess was proved right when I passed a concrete blockhouse, which hummed with the sound of an engine.

As I passed through the lines of neatly parked cars I heard a shout. 'You. Stop where you are.'

I stood still and raised my hands to show they were empty as two men armed with shotguns came out of a building and towards me. 'Who are you and what do you want?' said the taller of the men.

'To talk to someone,' I said. 'I haven't seen anyone sane for days.'

'Do you have The Death?' the shorter one demanded.

I shook my head.

'Are you sure? No coughing or sneezing or bleeding gums or back-side.'

'Quite sure,' I replied. 'I think I'm immune.'

'Are you armed?' The taller one again.

'Yes,' I replied.

'Let's see.'

I reached into my jacket with my fingertips and pulled out the Glock from under my arm by its butt.

'Put it on that car there,' said the tall man.

I did as I was told.

'Is that all?' said the shorter.

'Yes,' I lied.

'Come inside,' said the tall man as he collected my gun. 'It doesn't stink so bad in there.'

'I'd like that back,' I said.

'All in good time.'

They made me lead the way into the building and the automatic doors opened and closed for us. Once inside where it was true that the smell wasn't so bad, the shorter one frisked me. He was another amateur and missed the gun in my boot, just as months later Sid would do the same outside The Last Chance Saloon. I owed my life several times to having a gun in my boot. He found my knife, frowned, pulled it out of its scabbard and added it to his cache.

Once satisfied they took me into what must have been the manager's office and sat me down and offered me coffee.

38

THE COFFEE WAS SCUMMY, but they had cigarettes, which made up for it. 'Where you from?' asked the taller man who introduced himself as Don.

'London,' I replied.

'It's bad up there.'

I didn't know if it was a statement or a question. 'Very,' I said.

'Are you walking?'

'That's right. The roads are blocked.'

'You don't say. Where you heading?' The shorter one asked. His name was Vic.

'I don't know really,' I replied. 'I fancy the coast. It might be fresher down there. I reckon anywhere like this near all the bodies is asking for trouble. There's more diseases than just The Death.'

'But we're comfortable here,' said Don. 'We've got water and electricity. And food. And women. And there's easy pickings on the road.'

'How long's it all going to last though?' I said. 'I think we're going to have to get used to going without for a bit.'

'The Yanks'll be here soon,' said Vic optimistically.

'The Yanks,' I said. 'The last I heard it was worse over there.'

'No,' said Vic. 'They'll sort it, you just wait.'

He had more faith in the Americans than I did. 'Fair enough,' I said. 'But I think I'll be moving on. If I could just have my gun and knife back.'

Don smiled, and I'd seen a good deal of smiles like that in my old job, and I didn't like them. 'I don't think so,' he said. 'We're short of weapons here and this is a nice gun.'

'Maybe the Yanks'll bring you some,' I said, and regretted it as soon as I'd said it.

'Funny fella,' said Vic. 'Maybe we'd better put him in with the other one.'

'Good idea,' said Don and pointed my own gun at me.

Sod it. I knew I was better off by myself.

They hustled me through to some sort of storage area, opened a door, pushed me inside, slammed it shut and I heard the key turn. It was pitch black inside and I stood very still. I could hear breathing and said, 'hello' and someone flicked on a gas lighter.

It was Ugly, but I didn't know that then. All I did know was that the flame lit up a face that looked like a bear who'd been in a bad car crash. 'Who are you?' he growled.

'My name's John,' I replied. 'And it looks like we're cell mates.'

He laughed showing perfect white teeth. 'You told them to take a running jump too?'

'Something like that,' I replied, saw a table to one side and sat on it. 'You'd better save the gas,' I said and he let the flame go out leaving me with an afterimage in the blackness.

'So what's your story?' I asked.

'I'm a trucker,' he told me. 'Fuel oil. I managed to get here but can't get out again. Too many idiots dying on the road. They wanted my truck. I wanted different.'

'I don't think it makes a world of difference now,' I said. 'After what I've seen.'

'It was the way they asked,' he said. 'Impolite, at the point of a gun. Anyway they'll die here, the lot of them. I saw one who had something that wasn't The Death.'

'I told them the same. They didn't seem to like it much. They're expecting the Americans to arrive at any minute with aid parcels.'

'They're crazy. That bloke Don fancies himself king of the castle. They started talking about executing me.'

'I just wanted to leave, but they wouldn't give me my gun back.'

'See what I mean? Impolite.'

'But I've got another one.'

'You haven't.'

'Yes I have.'

He flicked on the gas again and said 'Show.'

I showed him the Glock. 'Perfect.' He looked at his watch. 'They'll bring in some grub soon. You want to get out of here?'

'Course.'

'I'll help.'

'Then what?' I asked.

'Then we'll leave.'

'Have they got any 4x4's?'

'Sure.'

'Then we'll take one and head across country. I'm going to make for the coast after that.'

'I'll string along if that's alright.'

'If you want,' I said. 'But I want my other pistol back first.'

'We'll get it. Don't worry about that.'

MY NEW FRIEND was right. Within ten minutes the door opened and Vic, shotgun at port arms, appeared with a woman in tow. She was carrying a tray with some greasy looking mess on two plates. The light hurt my eyes and I squinted up at the door. 'I think he's ill,' I said. The big man was lying on the floor beside me doubled up in pain and moaning gently.

'Is it The Death?' said Vic.

'I don't think so,' I said back.

He came over to us, perfectly silhouetting himself against the doorway. He knelt next to me, the barrel of his gun pointing harmlessly away and I stuck the Glock into his side. 'Put it down Vic and stay perfectly still.'

He did as he was told, and my new friend grabbed the gun and held it on him.

I got up and walked over to the woman who was still standing in the doorway. She had ginger hair pulled back in a ponytail and was wearing a check shirt and denims. 'Are you happy here?' I said.

She looked scared, but managed to shake her head.

'Then put that slop down and get lost.'

'Are you leaving?' she asked.

'In a bit.'

'Can I come with you?'

I was a bit taken aback at that. 'Are you sure?'

'I can cook better than this muck if you'll let me. I don't want to stay here. That Don's crazy. You should see what he's done.'

'What do you think?' I said over my shoulder.

My friend grinned. 'Sure. Why not. I'm always partial to a bit of female company. 'Specially one as good looking as her.'

'See what you'll have to put up with,' I said.

She smiled, and in fact she was prettier than I'd first thought. 'I can deal with a big ugly boy like that,' she said. 'I had four brothers.'

'I think you've got a fan,' I said to him. 'And she's right, you are damned ugly.' And in the light he was. 'What do I call you by the way.'

'Ugly'll do,' he said. And from there on in, Ugly it was.

SHE TOLD US her name was Sandy. 'Have you got anything you want to get?' I said to her.

She shook her head. 'Just myself,' she added.

'I want my other gun,' I said. 'We're going to need it. And a weapon for you, if you can use one.'

'I can,' she said.'

Then to Ugly. 'Take care of that fucker.'

He grinned in the gloom, took the shotgun by the barrel and swung it hard so that the butt hit Vic's head with a sickening crunch that meant brain damage at the best, death at the worst. 'I don't like being locked up,' he said to the unconscious man as he lay on the floor. 'I get claustrophobic.'

I made a mental note never to incarcerate the big man.

We went out into the empty corridor and Sandy locked the door behind us and pocketed the key. 'Where's the office?' I asked momentarily disorientated.

'Follow me,' she said and the three of us set off.

We hurried through the corridors, occasionally passing people who gave Ugly and me no more than cursory glances and who often greeted Sandy, who returned the greetings with an easy smile. I was glad she was with us to take the heat off.

When we came to the front of the building where the shops and restaurants had been there were more people about. 'Through here,' said Sandy. 'Quick.'

We pushed through a door and a man I hadn't seen before was lounging by the entrance to the office. When he saw us he stood up straight and raised the shotgun he was carrying, and Ugly blew half his torso off with his. 'Grab his gun,' I said to Sandy as I kicked open the office door to find Don sitting behind the desk a look of amazement on his face, my rucksack, Glock and knife on the desk in front of him. 'Don't,' I said as he went for the gun.

He sat back and raised his hands as I helped myself to the weapon and picked up my rucksack. 'So what are we going to do with you?' I said.

'Listen…' he stuttered.

'Shut it,' I ordered. 'I need to think.'

But my thoughts were interrupted as Sandy came into the room walked over to the desk, raised the gun she'd liberated and shot him in the head. The blast threw Don and his chair back against the wall.

'We couldn't leave him,' said Sandy. 'He was evil. Crazy. A lunatic.'

'Fair enough,' I said. 'And I see you do know how to use a gun. Now we need a vehicle. Where are they?'

'Come on,' she said. 'I'll show you.' and I followed her out of the office again where Ugly was covering the door with his gun.

'What happened?' he asked.

'Sandy solved the Don problem,' I told him. 'Come on, let's get out of here.'

Sandy led us away from the main concourse to a double door with push bars that let us out into the car park. There was a line of Range Rovers, Land Rovers, Suzukis and Toyota all terrain vehicles. I climbed behind the wheel of the nearest Land Rover. The keys were in the ignition. I gave them half a turn and the needle on the fuel gauge swung round to the 'F'. I tossed Ugly my knife. 'The tyres,' I said, and he ran along the line stabbing one tyre of each vehicle as I started the engine.

'They're coming,' yelled Sandy, as a crowd of men and women came running round the side of the building, carrying an assortment of firearms.

'Ugly.' I yelled. 'Let's go,' and I slammed the Land Rover into gear, ran it to where he was waiting, and came to a halt with a screech of rubber. He leapt into the seat beside me as bullets and shotgun pellets whistled past the car, only pausing to fire off the other barrel of the shotgun at the crowd which sent them diving to the ground.

Once he was inside I took off again, aimed the Land Rover's bonnet at the fence closest to us, smashed through it, down a dip, across a service road, through a wooden fence, across a field and away.

'In future,' I said to no one in particular 'I'm going to shoot first and ask questions afterwards.'

41

THE LAND ROVER slid and skidded across the field of grass and I slowed down as our pursuers vanished behind us, until eventually I forded a small stream and brought the truck to a halt on the far bank. 'Everyone OK?' I asked anxiously. I'd heard a couple of those bullets whack into the bodywork of the car.

'Sure,' said Ugly.

'All in one piece,' said Sandy from the back.

'Right,' I said. 'My plan was to make for the coast and fresh air. Is that alright with you two?'

Ugly shrugged.

'Sounds as good a plan as any,' said Sandy.

'OK,' I said. 'Let's go.'

We headed south, but after the experience at the M25 services I tried as much as possible to keep off road. It was quite easy as long as I forgot about such niceties as fences and property lines. Those were a thing of the past, and the Land Rover destroyed them with ease. We filled up with petrol at a little garage in a tiny village in Surrey as the sun set. Ugly found the manual handle for the pumps and raised the fuel by hand. I would've had no idea. It was handy having a trucker on board. He looked at the engine of the Land Rover and declared it to be OK. I took that to be fine praise.

Then we looked for somewhere to sleep, which was when we met Brenda and Gwen.

The garage had also been a general store, and although the contents had been pretty well looted there were still some tins and packets of food which we loaded into the back of the truck. 'We need to find somewhere to stay the night,' I said when that was done. 'I'm not going to risk driving in the dark.'

Sandy had noticed a sign for a hotel at the last turn off and we decided to try it. 'At least there'll be plenty of beds,' she said.

'And maybe they'll be full of bodies,' said Ugly.

'Let's try it and see,' I said and pointed the Land Rover in that direction.

The sign led to a twisty lane that opened onto a drive through double gates and terminated in a gravel lot where a couple of dusty cars that had an abandoned look were parked.

We climbed out of the truck as the sun dipped below the eaves of the hotel; a massive building that had probably once been the local manor house. 'A country house hotel,' I said. 'Whoever thought I'd ever stay in one of those again?'

'It looks like something out of a horror film to me,' remarked Sandy.

'It is,' I replied. 'And we're all starring in it.'

The front doors were unlocked and we pushed through into the silence of the foyer with our guns in our hands. It was dark and gloomy inside and the air had the faint odour of a thousand past meals served.

'Seems quiet enough,' I said. 'Let's take a look round.'

'I'll see if the bar's open,' said Ugly, as Sandy and I took the wide flight of stairs to the first floor.

We went all the way up to the top of the building and checked the rooms coming back down. There were no bodies to be found, but a couple of the rooms, although deserted had recently been slept in.

We headed back to the ground floor and went looking for Ugly. He was sitting in the massive, deserted bar sipping beer from a bottle. 'Hello folks,' he said. 'Good here, eh?'

'Not bad,' I replied. 'Someone's been here recently.'

'Someone's here now,' he said.

'Who?'

'The cook. She's in the back getting something ready for our dinner. And there's a barmaid too. Oi, Gwen,' he shouted. 'How about a couple more beers out here for my friends.'

The door behind the bar opened and a young woman in a denim shirt poked her head through. 'Sure Ugly,' she said. Then to me and Sandy. 'Good evening. It'll be good to have some guests again.' And with a quick smile she vanished back from whence she'd come.

I LOOKED AT UGLY in amazement. 'What's all that about?' I said.

'Gwen and Brenda,' he said. 'Chief cook and bottlewasher at The Grange Hotel.'

Sandy gave him the snake's eye.

'Don't worry love,' he said. 'They're not interested in me or John, but they might be in you.'

'Do what?' she asked.

'Lesbians,' he explained.

'How do you know?' I said. 'You've only been here for ten minutes and you've got their life story already.'

He shrugged. 'It comes natural,' he said. 'I have great empathy with women, animals and engines.'

'So I've noticed,' said Sandy.

I saw what he meant. They'd only been acquainted for a day and already she was putting up 'Hands Off' signs. 'Children, children,' I said. 'Play nice.'

At that point Gwen came back in with two bottles of beer. 'They've been in the cold room.' she said. 'There's no power, but it's chilly in there and they should be quite cool. Nothing worse than warm beer I always say.'

She flicked off the tops of the bottles and lined them up in front of Sandy and me. 'You must be John,' she said. 'And you're Sandy. It's nice to see some life around the old place. Brenda'll be in a minute. She's just mashing some potatoes.'

I sat on a bar stool and raised the bottle to my lips. It tasted delicious, not freezing, but pleasantly cool. 'Lovely,' I said. 'I've always been fond of mashed potatoes.'

Brenda introduced herself a little while later. She was a very big woman dressed in denims too, and as she came into the bar she pushed a lock of hair off her sweaty forehead. 'Evening,' she said. 'Welcome to The Grange. I'm glad you found us.'

We might just have been a trio of guests here for a long week-end who got lost on the way. 'Good evening,' I said back.

All five of us sat down to dinner ten minutes later in the dining room lit by candles. It was a feast after the way I'd eaten for the past week or so. The starter was tomato soup with crackers. Then frankfurters with mashed potatoes and a choice of three vegetables followed by tinned fruit and cream, and black coffee with brandy. Red wine was served throughout the meal. After we'd finished Gwen brought cigars and Ugly and I puffed away as we all drank port and Brenda told her and Gwen's story.

43

THEY'D BOTH BEEN WORKING at the hotel. Brenda as the assistant chef, Gwen handling general duties. Anything from loading the washing-up machine to cleaning the rooms with a little bartending on the side. Brenda had been there for a number of years, Gwen arriving more recently. They'd discovered each other's sexual predilections and become lovers. Everything was fine as long as they were discreet and they'd been very happy.

Then The Death came. One by the one the staff and guests had succumbed, until eventually only the pair of them were left. This had taken a matter of weeks, the two women taking over more and more of the chores of the hotel as it happened. The villagers had died too, or left looking for pastures new and safer. Eventually they were left with ten dead bodies at The Grange and the village was empty.

'We gave the dead a decent burial at the back of the orchard,' explained Brenda. 'It was hard work but we managed.'

When the power went off, the food in the deep freeze spoiled, but there was a large of quantity of canned and freeze-dried edibles in storage, and an old fashioned wood burning stove in the kitchen where Brenda cooked. The wine cellars and beer and liquor stores were still intact and they simply decided to stay and live off what they had.

Apart from the cars parked out front the hotel had one old van which they used to transport as many provisions as they could carry from the village until it ran out of fuel and what petrol they could siphon from the cars. They didn't have Ugly's knowledge of petrol pumps to extract more petrol from the underground tanks.

'You were lucky you were both immune,' I said. 'You know what's happened in the outside world.'

'Not since the radio and TV went off,' replied Brenda. 'But we imagined the worst.'

'Multiply it by ten,' I said. 'And you might have some idea.

The people that survived The Death are busy killing each other off for what they can scavenge off the bodies.'

'But you're not like that,' said Gwen.

'But we might've been,' I replied.

'Not him,' she said, looking at Ugly. 'He's kind.'

I remembered how he'd tried to take Vic's head off with the butt of his shotgun and smiled to myself at her naivete. 'When he's in the mood,' I said.

'We could stay here too,' suggested Sandy. 'If Brenda and Gwen don't mind.'

I shook my head. 'This place will be too big to heat in the winter. I take it there's no emergency power supply,' I said to Brenda.

She shook her head.

'And we're too close to the motorway and those people there.' Ugly had explained how we'd met over the entree. 'Not that I think they'll last long. It took us the best part of a day to get here cross country, but if the roads are anything like clear and they come looking they could be here within an hour, and I certainly don't want them to find us. This place is well signposted and if anyone's looking for supplies it'll be an obvious choice. Maybe not now, but sometime soon people are going to start coming down that road and they might not all be as friendly as we are.'

I saw fear in Brenda's eyes for a second and she nodded agreement.

'No,' I went on. 'I think my idea's best. Head for the coast and scout out a remote house with a generator that we can defend. That's the best plan, and I intend to get going in the morning. Ugly and Sandy, you can come with me, or stay here just as you like.'

'I'm with him,' said Ugly.'

'And I'm with you,' chorused Sandy.

'Could we come with you?' ventured Brenda after a moment's silence.

'The way you cook you'd be an asset,' I said. 'But Christ knows what we're going to find down the road. It's murder out there literally. Maybe no one will come here and you'll be safe forever.'

'Forever's a long time,' said Brenda. 'If you'll have us we'll come. Gwen?'

Her friend nodded agreement.

'OK. Here's what we'll do,' I said. 'We'll put some petrol in that van of yours and load it up with as much food that won't perish as it'll take and hide it in the woods. I'd take it with us but we need four wheel drive. Anyway it won't hurt to have supply dumps here and there. We might be grateful of them some day. Then we'll put as much as we can of the rest in the Land Rover and take off. The quicker we get a base to operate from the better. Agreed?'

All four of my companions nodded and we filled our glasses and toasted our plan.

44

THAT NIGHT I SLEPT IN A BED for the first time in I didn't know how long. We all did. I think Ugly and Sandy took the honeymoon suite but I didn't like to ask.

The next morning we loaded the two vehicles with as much as they could take from the food and wine supplies, put some petrol in the hotel van and I drove it deep into the woods and camouflaged it with branches cut from the trees. When I returned everyone else was ready to go.

We crammed ourselves into the Land Rover, drove back to village, topped up the tank and filled some cans with gas for emergencies. Then we headed south again.

There was a holiday atmosphere inside the truck but I kept one of my pistols tucked down the back of my seat just in case the worst happened.

And of course it did.

That day I took the risk of driving on proper roads, although I stuck as much as possible to the tiniest of lanes working on the assumption that there would have been less traffic on them, and subsequently less chance of them being blocked.

But of course when they were blocked they were blocked completely and half a dozen times I had to reverse the Land Rover until I found a gate into a field so that I could bypass the blockage, or else force it though a hedge or fence to manage it, which took time and effort because I didn't want to do any damage to the truck.

After the fourth or fifth diversion we stopped to lunch by a fast running stream. 'This is going to take forever,' I said.

'We've got nothing but time,' said Ugly who was getting to be a bit of a philosopher. 'It's not a problem.'

'I just want to find somewhere permanent for us,' I replied. 'The longer we're on the road the more chance there is of something going wrong.'

How right I was.

The next half hour or so was uneventful until I passed a sign-post for a village named Stavely, swung the truck round a bend in the road and was faced by a barricade of cars, topped by the red and white flag of St. George and a shot rang out and the windscreen of the Land Rover starred.

I jammed on the brakes and the truck skidded to a halt with a screech of tyres and the smell of burning rubber and Ugly, sitting in the passenger seat punched out the glass and yelled 'Back up!'

I jammed the gear stick into reverse and with another yelp from the tyres careened backwards only to see in the mirror a car pulling across the road behind us, neatly boxing us in.

I hit the brakes again and as the Land Rover stopped three men stepped into the road, one from behind the car and two from behind the barricades.

'Get out of the car with your hands up,' shouted one of them, a middle aged man with a military bearing, wearing a Barbour and green wellingtons and carrying a rifle, who appeared to be the leader.

I looked at Ugly and he looked back. 'Better do it,' I said. 'We're caught in the crossfire here.'

All five of us did as we were told and stood in the roadway as the three men approached. 'Are you armed?' asked the leader.

'There's a couple of shotguns and a pistol in the car,' I said.

'Search them,' said the leader.

The other two men, one a teenager, and the other somewhere in his thirties both with shotguns of their own did his bidding, giving the women an especially close search and they found my other Glock and my knife.

'Welcome to the independent state of Stavely,' said the leader. 'My name is Colonel Williams and my young friends are Jack Holmes,' he pointed to the teenage boy. 'And Mark Stacey.'

'Why did you shoot at us?' I asked mildly. 'You could've killed someone.'

'That was Jack,' he said. 'His first taste of action. I'm afraid he was rather precipitous. My apologies. Jack…'

'Yeah sorry,' said the boy.

I looked at Ugly and saw in his eyes that the boy would be even sorrier if he ever got him on his own.

'You have some fine weapons here,' said Williams. 'Were you military?'

'Police,' I said.

It was the first time I'd said anything about my past and I saw the surprise in my new friend's eyes.

'Splendid,' said Williams. 'Just what we need.'

'We?' I asked.

'The local government we've set up here from the survivors of the nearest villages. There's not many of us, but we have new recruits every day.'

'At gunpoint,' I said.

'Sorry,' said Williams lowering his rifle and indicating that the other two do the same. 'Now can I count on you for support?'

45

'MAYBE,' I SAID. 'But what's in it for us?'

'Excellent,' said Williams. 'Perhaps if we adjourned to the pub we could talk about it. Then to his cohorts. 'You two. Watch the road. And get this vehicle behind the barricades.'

'Yes sir,' they chorused like good little soldiers, and I caught Ugly's eye again and gave him a cynical smile.

The Colonel led us between the cars in front of our truck, and after a short walk we came into the village proper and he led us towards a pub called the Dog and Duck and inside its cool bar area. 'Stanley,' he called when we got through the door, and a fat, fiftyish bloke with a balding head stepped through from the back of the pub.

'Yes Colonel sir,' he said.

'What'll you have?' the colonel inquired of our party.

'Got any beer?' asked Ugly.

'Of course,' replied Stanley. 'We always kept ale in the wood.'

'A pint then,' said Ugly.

'Same for me,' said Brenda.

'Any lager?' asked Sandy.

'Some bottles,' replied the barman.

'That'll do,' she said.

'Make it two,' said Gwen.

'I'll have a brandy,' I said.

'And I'll join him,' said Williams.

When we were all seated with our drinks of choice and we'd all introduced ourselves, Williams said. 'You asked what's in it for you. Well I'll tell you. We desperately need fresh blood here. We need to scavenge the local area for food and fuel. And trade with other settlements, of which I'm sure there'll be many. We have meat on the hoof and vegetables in the ground, but precious few who can care for them.'

'I can,' said Brenda.

'Splendid,' he said.

'And?' I inquired.

'And whoever's here at the beginning will end up ruling the roost,' said Williams. 'Civilisation will return, and those in at the start of it will end up with the power.'

'How many of you are there so far?' I asked.

'Fifteen. Twenty including you.'

I shook my head. 'Hardly an independent state,' I said. 'More like a gang.'

'The journey of a thousand miles starts with a single step,' he said.

'How true,' I replied. 'But we're happy as we are.'

'And where were you going?'

'We've been heading for the coast.'

'But why?'

'It was just an idea of mine since I left London.'

'Be reasonable man,' said Williams. 'There's strength in numbers.'

'But I'm not sure I want to take orders from anyone again. I've had my fill of that,' I said. 'Although I don't know about the others.'

'I'm sure we could come to some arrangement...' Williams' voice took on a wheedling tone.

'No,' I said. 'It's not for me. I'd like to move on.'

Williams appealed to the other four.

One by one they told him they'd rather stick with me and continue our journey.

As they were speaking I saw Williams raise an eyebrow to the man behind the bar and he vanished like smoke.

'So if we can just have our weapons and truck we'll be off,' I said when they'd finished talking. 'But we know where you are and when we're settled we could trade with you.'

'I'm sorry,' said Williams. 'You can go but your belongings stay.'

Ugly made as if to reach across the table and grab him, when we heard the click of weapons being cocked and from the shadows at the corner of the bar half a dozen figures appeared with rifles and shotguns at the ready.

46

'**VERY HOSPITABLE**,' I said. 'What do you do now? Execute us?'

'We're not that uncivilised,' replied Williams. 'We just keep your stuff and let you go.'

'Everything?' I inquired, fixing Ugly with a look that said 'do nothing.'

'Everything I'm afraid,' said Williams. 'Our need is greater than yours.'

'In your opinion,' I retorted but to no avail.

'Anyone of you that wants can still stay,' he added. 'You're very welcome.'

None of our party bothered to reply.

'Very well,' he said. 'We'll escort you out of the village.'

'Don't you mean the independent state?' I asked, but he didn't bother to reply.

We were led outside at gunpoint, passing what looked like a brand new seven seater, long wheelbase Land Rover with a winch mounted on the front and spare wheel hoisted high on its back door.

'This way,' ordered Williams, and still with guns at our back we walked down the main street of the village to another barricade of cars also decorated with the English flag. 'Just keep walking, and don't come back' he said. 'You'll find a new car and food sooner or later. There's plenty to be had.'

'You're too thoughtful,' I said as we went through the barricade and up a slight hill until we were out of sight.

'Fucking good job,' said Ugly. 'What do we do now?'

'That's the second time some chancer has taken my weapons off me,' I said. 'I'm getting tired of it. I'm going back to get them, and that Land Rover that was parked outside the boozer. We can use that.'

'But we're unarmed,' said Gwen. 'And won't they expect that?'

'If they'd've expected that they'd've killed us,' I said. 'They're still civilised. I'm not. If you want to go on I'll understand. It'll be dangerous to go back, but worth it.'

'And what do we do with them?' Asked Brenda.

'Kill them all,' I said. 'Just like they should've done to us.'

'But there's women there,' protested Gwen.

That was the first time I used the expression that was to become our motto. Christ knows where it came from. Some old film maybe, or a book, or maybe just out of my scrambled brain. 'Kill them all and let God sort them out,' I said. 'Now who's coming with me?'

47

NONE OF THE OTHER FOUR made a move and I said. 'We'd better find somewhere to rest until it gets dark. It's going to be a busy night.'

We pushed on for about a quarter of a mile until we came to the entrance to a small wood. 'This'll do,' I said. 'Try and get some sleep.'

We lay down on the soft grass in a clearing and I dozed off but I kept dreaming of my family and eventually I decided to go for a walk, leaving the others. I strolled along through the wood until I found a well used path that led up to a small house. The front door was closed up tight so I went round the back and broke a window in the kitchen and climbed through.

The place smelled of death and I found a bloated body sitting in an armchair in the living room. Flies swarmed round the body and I wrinkled my nose in disgust.

I went through the rest of the house from top to bottom as the sun set outside. In one of the drawers in a bureau close to the body I discovered a sheath knife with a good point on it, and upstairs a BB gun in the shape of an old Colt .45 automatic. I loaded the gun with pellets and went back to find my companions.

It was twilight when I got back to the clearing.

'This could come in useful,' I said, showing them the gun. 'In the dark it'll look like the real thing. And this is for you Ugly.' I tossed him the knife and he unsheathed it and tested the point with his thumb.

'I'm hungry,' said Sandy.

'We'll eat later,' I said. 'If any of us survive. Otherwise it'd just be a waste of good food. That is if we had any.'

When it was full dark, we walked in single file back the way we'd come, this time staying off the road. The barricade we'd passed through was lit with hurricane lamps and I saw that there were two guards on duty. 'Me and Ugly will take care of these two, ' I said. 'Then you join us. Fifteen in all,' I reminded my companions. 'And I want to see fifteen bodies at the end.'

Taking opposite sides of the road Ugly and I crept down towards the barricade. When we got up close I could hear the sound of voices. I popped my head up and saw the two men facing each other, both leaning against the wing of a car. One held a pump action shotgun, the other a rifle. I saw Ugly's face white against the darkness of the hedge opposite and I stepped into the men's view holding the BB gun in my fist. 'Put your weapons down,' I said. 'And not a sound.'

The surprise of my approach stunned them for a second, just long enough for Ugly to come up behind the one with the shotgun and sink the knife into his back, twist it and pull it out, catching the man's gun as he dropped it, before he buckled at the knees and fell. The one with the rifle turned the gun in Ugly's direction and opened his mouth to shout, and I clubbed him with the air gun I was holding. It wasn't a very powerful weapon, but it weighed the same as the pistol it replicated, and it bounced off his skull with a satisfying clang and he joined his friend on the tarmac.

'Kill that one,' I said to Ugly, indicating the one I'd hit. 'And make sure the other one's dead.'

Ugly grinned and did as he was told and I stood up and waved to the women.

They joined us in a second, and Ugly picked up the rifle and checked the clip, whilst I racked the shells through the pump. Five in all, and another five in the dead man's pocket. I carefully reloaded.

'Give me that knife,' said Brenda. 'I've done some butchering.'

'Fine,' said Ugly and handed it over.

'You're with us Brenda,' I said. 'You two,' to Sandy and Gwen. 'Stay out of sight here. When we've got more weapons we'll come back. If you hear any shooting come get us.'

The girls nodded and slid into the shadows by the hedge, and Ugly, Brenda and I started off down the street.

The pub was lit with more lanterns but we ignored it and went on to the first barricade we'd come to that afternoon, passing our windscreenless truck still full of the boxes we'd loaded it with that morning on the way. There were two guards on duty there also. One woman one man. Brenda walked boldly up and stabbed the woman in the throat, whilst Ugly battered the man to the ground with the butt of his rifle. He was getting quite good at that.

Four down, eleven to go, and two double barrelled shotguns and a score or so of shells to add to our arsenal.

48

WE CARRIED THE NEW WEAPONS back to the other barricade, and gave one shotgun and a handful of shells each to Sandy and Gwen. Brenda kept hold of the knife. Then all together we returned to the pub.

The first thing I did was to check out the new Land Rover that still sat outside. The truck was unlocked and the keys were in the ignition. I checked the fuel situation. It was full. I smiled, gestured for the others to join me, let off the handbrake, and we pushed the motor further down the road. If there were going to be bullets flying I didn't want the truck damaged. After that I peered through the window of the building and saw the barman from earlier standing behind the counter, and six people sitting at the bar with glasses in front of them. Five women and one man. Williams wasn't with them, and I'd've bet my boots that he would have my pair of Glocks. Guns befitting of his status as leader of this little republic of his.

I passed on the information in a whisper to the rest and posted the women to watch the pub whilst Ugly and I checked the rest of the village.

There were a few cottages with lamps or candles burning and we crept around peeping inside. Inside the first one we came to was a lone woman sitting, reading by candlelight. At the second the room was empty, but at the third we hit pay-dirt. Williams was inside talking to two men. I tapped on the door with the butt of my shotgun as Ugly covered the window from outside.

Williams himself answered and I put the gun to his throat one handed, my finger on the trigger and I covered my mouth with the forefinger of the other to signify that he should be silent. His face was a picture of shocked surprise.

'Outside,' I said and when he concurred I clubbed him to the ground. He was carrying one of my Glocks in my shoulder holster under his arm. The other was in his belt. I relieved him of both and was undoing the holster when a voice from inside said, 'Colonel' and one of Williams' companions appeared at the door. He was carrying an old

Webley army revolver.

I fired the shotgun into his face at point-blank range and his head left his body and rolled down the passage.

Ugly fired his rifle through the window twice and I heard a thud from inside the building, then a confusion of shouts from the direction of the pub. Followed by the explosions of more shotgun rounds.

'Come on,' I shouted to Ugly. 'We'd better help the girls.' But before I went I wasted a precious 9mm round on Williams to finish him off.

As we raced round the corner from Williams' house, the woman I'd seen reading through her window appeared at her door, book still in hand. I shot her in the stomach with the pump.

There was a firefight at the pub when we got there and we were winning. The girls had waited for the people inside to come out when they heard the shots, and three of them were lying on the small turnaround in front of the pub where the Land Rover had been parked.

Ugly and I slid to a halt beside them dodging the sporadic fire from inside the Dog and Duck. 'There's at least three more inside,' I said. 'We can't waste time and ammunition here. We'll burn them out.'

'How?' said Brenda.

'Easy. Wait here,' I replied.

I ran back to our old Land Rover, opened the back and pulled out a couple of the bottles of wine we'd packed. I whacked the tops off on the bumper, poured the wine into the gutter and found the rubber hose we'd brought with us in case we had to siphon petrol en route and opened up the tank. I got a mouthful of petrol, spat it out and filled them, then tore strips of cloth from my shirt and forced them into the tops of the bottles. I ran back to where my friends were waiting, sent Ugly and Gwen round to cover the back door, took out my lighter, lit the material, yelled 'Cover me,' jumped up and ran towards the pub. When I was close enough I lobbed the bottles through the front window and watched as the inside of the building lit up.

It wasn't long before the pub was burning merrily and people started to evacuate. We shot them down like dogs.

And so ended the battle for the independent state of Stavely.

49

WE LEFT THE BODIES where they lay and found beds where we could, and I lay awake shaking with tension from the battle with the flames from the burning pub playing on my eyelids.

The next morning we collected the bodies, lay them together on the road, doused them with petrol and set them alight.

As we were loading up our new transport with the contents of the Land Rover we'd arrived in, and the weapons and ammunition we'd taken from the corpses I heard a rustling in the hedge at the side of the road and swung round drawing and cocking the Glock in my belt as I did so. 'Come out,' I shouted. 'Or I'll shoot.'

There was more rustling and a bedraggled looking little dog wormed its way onto the blacktop and came and sniffed my boots.

'Be careful,' said Ugly who was standing next to me. 'She might be armed.'

'Funny' I said. 'And how do you know it's a she?' And bent down and stroked the back of the dog's head. 'What's up puppy?' I said. 'Did we kill your master? Are you lost?'

'I think we all are,' said Ugly, and stroked the dog's undersides exposing her nipples 'And I told you about my affinity with animals.'

'Clever,' I said, and the dog rubbed itself against my leg.

'Sure looks like you've made a friend,' said Ugly.

'No way,' I said. 'I've got enough problems with you lot.'

But the dog wouldn't go away and when the girls started to fuss over her I said. 'Don't get attached. We're leaving it behind.'

As soon as I spoke the dog looked at me with liquid eyes and licked my hand.

'No chance,' I said to her.

When we were ready to go the dog wouldn't leave me alone and eventually I had to push her away from the Land Rover as we all got on board.

I switched on, put the truck into gear and pulled away, but as I looked in the rear view mirror I saw the dog sitting on the white line that ran down the middle of the road with its ears flat against its head and such a dejected look on its face that it touched me deep inside.

With a sigh I put on the brakes, put the truck into neutral, opened the door and called. 'Hey Puppy.'

The dog's ears pricked up and it ran towards me and jumped up into my arms and everyone inside the vehicle clapped as I got behind the wheel again, and with the dog on my lap drove on.

So that's how Puppy came into my life.

We kept on driving south and reached the coast road in the afternoon and began looking for our new home.

It took us two days, and in that time we saw no other sign of human life.

Eventually, just outside Lewes, Ugly, who was driving, turned the truck down yet another unmarked road until it opened up into a clear space on the cliff top and for the first time we saw the ranch-style dwelling that we were to make our base camp.

It was painted white with a red tile roof, and there was an empty swimming pool at the back with a cabana style changing room. At the back of the house was a flower garden going to seed, with a large vegetable patch and a greenhouse.

'This looks promising,' I said.

'I wonder if anyone's home?' said Ugly.

'Only one way to find out.'

Ugly stopped the truck about a hundred yards from the house and we all dismounted, weapons at the ready and Puppy ran and took a wee in the flower garden.

'She seems happy enough,' said Ugly. 'I think she'd know if there was anyone about. Animals do.'

'I'll take your word for it,' I replied, still not entirely happy with becoming a pet owner.

We checked the house and it was deserted except for the body of the owner. It was massive, with seven bedrooms. There was a huge kitchen at the back looking out over the gardens to the sea. The grounds were deserted too, except for half a dozen chickens in a hen house back beyond the greenhouse who'd managed to stay alive foraging for themselves. Brenda came out of the chicken coop blowing a stray feather off her chin and told us that there were dozens of eggs rotting away inside. Meanwhile Gwen reported that there was a fresh water stream just a dozen or so yards away inside the woods that came right up to the garden. The house had water pipes coming in but of course they were dry, but there was no sewage outlet, the place being so remote. Instead there was a septic tank that Ugly checked and told us was in working order. But the best thing was that attached to the cabana was a generator housing with a petrol engine that Ugly fired up first time of trying, and all the lights in the house worked.

'Better and better,' said Ugly when he'd got the motor running smoothly. 'All the comforts of home.

'So what do you say?' I asked when we were all gathered together by the side of the empty pool.

'I don't think we'll find anywhere better,' said Brenda, 'and there's an Aga cooker in the kitchen so we don't need power to cook.'

'So is this it?' I asked and one by one my companions assented.

'Welcome home then,' I said. 'And no fighting over the rooms.'

50

'SO THAT'S HOW WE GOT HERE,' I said to Loretta. The moon had moved around the sky as I told the story and the first signs of dawn were visible in the east.

'And where did Pansy come from?'

'She'd had a rough time,' I told her. 'We met her on the road a month or so after we arrived here. She was half dead and Ugly saved her.'

'Quite a story,' she said.

'And now you're here too.'

She nodded and her eyes glistened in the gloom.

'So tell me about this petrol run,' I said.

'I've already told you.'

'Have you been on it?'

She nodded and touched her stomach. 'The father of my baby was one of the outriders. He took me once on the back of his bike. When Marco found out he had him killed.'

'The more I hear about Marco the more I want to fuck him over,' I said.

'The people who go on the run are a hard bunch.'

'And you think we aren't?'

'But there's so few of you.'

'We've managed so far. Will you help us?'

'How?'

'You know the route they take. You know where the refinery is. You can show us the roads they take and we can work out the best place to lay an ambush. If you're going to stay here it would be nice to have heat and light all winter. Having a baby is a risky business under the circumstances you're in with no doctor or midwife. We haven't got enough fuel to run the generator for more than a few hours at a time. With two tankers full we could run it all winter. At least then we'd have hot water.'

'And clean towels just like in the cowboy films.'

'Something like that. But seriously. We don't know if your baby is going to be immune. Or if The Death's still around. In fact we know precious little.'

'I'm sorry to be such a nuisance.'

'You're not.'

'And you'll help me if I help you?'

'Of course. We'd help you anyway.'

'You're good people.'

'I don't think there's any such thing anymore. We're killers all of us. Stone cold killers. When we die we go straight to hell.'

'I doubt that. You do what you have to do. You do your best.'

'We try.'

'But you won't let me in your bed. I know I'm not your wife and I never could be, but I could try.'

'I'm not a good bet for a husband,' I replied. 'I let my last wife and child die.'

'From The Death?'

I nodded. How come I was telling her when I'd been determined not to.

'Then it wasn't your fault,' she said.

'But it certainly feels like it. I watched them die and buried them in our back garden.'

She got out of her seat and came and sat at the foot of my bed. 'You shouldn't feel that way. My family are dead too. Well at least I think they are. My mother and father and two sisters and a brother. And all my aunties and uncles and grandparents. But I don't know for sure what happened to them. They could still be alive. That's the worst part. I was away from home when The Death came. There were no phones, no transport. Nothing. I'll probably never know. At least you buried your family.'

She started to cry then, and it was just like when I'd looked in the mirror and seen Puppy. I knew I was being manipulated but I didn't care. 'Loretta,' I said.

'What?'

'Come to bed sweetheart, you must be exhausted, I know I am.'

And she did, and she felt so soft and warm in my arms that I felt the tears running down my face as I held her.

But for the first time since I'd buried Dominique and Louisa they weren't bitter tears of pain but cleansing tears of joy.

51

THE NEXT MORNING we were the last down to breakfast. The others were gathered round the table and all conversation ceased when we came in, Puppy bringing up the rear.

Ugly grinned. 'I heard there was a bit of midnight creeping,' he remarked.

I could feel myself redden. This had never happened before. 'Shut up,' I said.

'A very good morning to you too John,' he went on. 'I trust you slept well. And you too Loretta of course.'

Loretta was blushing too. 'John was telling me how you lot met,' she said.

'Besides other things of course,' said Brenda, and everyone at the table giggled.

'I'm obviously going to get no sense out of you lot this morning,' I said grumpily, helping myself to tea. 'Do you fancy a walk by the sea, Loretta?'

'Romantic,' said Ugly. 'Just make sure you don't fall in.'

The banter went on until Loretta and I had eaten and we could escape. 'Sorry about that,' I said as we walked hand in hand to the edge of the cliff with Puppy behind us, and I showed her the narrow path down to the shingle beach below.

'I don't mind,' she said. 'It's only because they love you. You've been alone all this time haven't you?'

I nodded as I lit a cigarette and let the breeze whip the smoke from my mouth.

'It's not good for you. You can get too involved in killing.'

'That's all I've seen for months until you came along.'

'And I've got life inside me. Do you mind?'

'Mind what?'

'That it's not yours.'

'Of course not. It's yours isn't it?'

'Some men would.'

'I'm not some men.'

'You can say that again,' and she cuddled up to me and we watched as the sea birds hovered over the white caps, picking food from the great sea and Puppy gambolled along the beach trying to work out why she couldn't fly.

We were gone for about two hours and when we got back to the house everyone but Brenda was lounging around in the living room. 'Where's Bren?' I asked.

'In the kitchen,' said Gwen. 'Where I should be. It's my turn to cook.'

'Give her a shout will you?' I asked. 'That can wait. We need to talk first.'

When Brenda joined us I said. 'I've been talking to Loretta.'

There were a few giggles and I said. 'Shut up. This is serious.'

When they were quiet I went on. 'She knows where the petrol refinery is where Marco gets his fuel, and the route his men take to get there. She's going to show us and we're going to take those tankers off them.'

There were looks of amazement all round and Ugly made as to speak but I stopped him with a gesture. 'I suggest we start tomorrow morning and work out our plan when we get to Essex. Now we haven't been up that way for a while and we don't know what we're going to find. It's going to be dangerous, but if we can pull it off it'll be worth it. We'll have fuel to last us the winter. When we get back Ugly and I can go off scavenging for food again, and with a bit of luck we'll be able to hunker down here when the weather gets bad and spend a comfortable few months without any worries. Then when the spring comes we can see what's become of the human race in our absence. Now what do you say?'

'I think it's madness,' said Loretta.

'Me too,' agreed Ugly, and I looked at him in amazement, until his face split into a big beam and he added, 'I can't wait.'

'Funny,' I said. 'What about the rest of you?'

There were murmurs of assent from everyone in the room.

'Loretta?' I said.

She shook her head. 'Looks like I'm out voted,' she said.

I smiled. 'Good. Now it's going to be a long drive. We're going to have to bypass London to the west and head east across the top.'

'No,' interrupted Pansy. 'No we won't.'

'What?' I said.

'We forgot to tell you. We heard the radio.'

'What are you talking about?' I thought she'd temporarily lost her senses, but Gwen and Brenda and Sandy were nodding in agreement.

'While you were gone the last time I was playing around with the radio,' Patsy explained. 'We heard a station. We meant to tell you but there was so much excitement last night what with Loretta and everything.'

'What station?' I asked.

Brenda took up the story. 'They called themselves Radio England,' she said. 'Broadcasting from Kent somewhere. From a pirate transmitter they'd found. They were only on for a couple of hours one Sunday night. Playing music. But they said that the Dartford Tunnel was open. And if anyone wants to use it they have to pay a toll.'

I was amazed. 'What kind of toll?'

'Anything. Food, drink, petrol. Anything useful.'

'Jesus,' I said. 'A radio station. It'll be *Top Of The Pops* next. Have you heard it since?'

The four women shook their heads. 'No. It was very faint. Maybe it was just a fluke it reached this far,' said Brenda.

'Do you remember the frequency?'

'Sure,' said Pansy. 'One-four-nine on FM.'

'Dartford Tunnel's open,' I said. 'God that could save us days of travel. It's an omen. A good one. But we mustn't underestimate the danger we're going to put ourselves in,' I went on. 'There's going to be fifteen or sixteen armed men guarding that convoy and they won't give it up easily. We might not all make it back here, and I'll understand if anyone doesn't want to come.

There'll be no recriminations. We're all friends here and I intend to keep it that way. So if anyone want to stay, say so now.'

There was silence.

'Good,' I said with a smile. 'I thought as much. Now we'll need food for the journey, so Brenda you're in charge. Ugly and I will check the weapons and the truck. Right let's get on with it, we've got a lot to do.'

We spent the rest of the day preparing for our quest. Ugly and I cleaned and loaded all the weapons except for Pansy's rifle which she insisted on looking after herself. 'That's my girl,' said Ugly.

When we'd loaded the clips for two of the two machine guns we'd liberated from The Last Chance Saloon I said to him. 'Ever fired one of these?'

He shook his head.

'Well you'd better. I was trained on an H&K so you'd better take the Uzi. I think we can spare thirty rounds, but don't waste them.'

I took him out into the woods and put the clip into the gun. 'Try it on single shot first,' I said.

He set the lever, then aimed the machine pistol at a small tree and popped off a few rounds. When I checked, they'd found their mark. 'Good,' I said. 'Very good.' When I was clear I said. 'Put it on to auto.' He did so. 'Now go.'

He emptied the clip in a few seconds, and strips of bark and wood flew off the little tree until when his magazine was spent the trunk teetered and fell to one side. 'You'll do,' I said.

We went back to the house and I cleaned and loaded the Uzi again whilst Ugly checked the Land Rover and filled spare cans with gas. I took three of the grenades we'd stolen from Marco and hooked them onto my gun belt. I felt like Batman. I also set aside a dozen sets of handcuffs I'd liberated from a police station on our travels. Two pairs each. If we ended up with prisoners they would come in handy. Whilst we were busy we set the radio to one-four-nine on the FM band but all we got was a static filled hiss.

As Ugly was stowing the weapons into the back of the truck I went and found Brenda and Gwen in the kitchen.

'Everything alright?' I asked.

'Very good,' said Brenda. 'I'm taking food for a week. OK? And a box of wine and food for the tunnel toll each way.'

'Excellent.' I said. 'God knows how long we'll be gone. I just hope it wasn't a hoax, otherwise we'll be screwed. We'll have to come all the way back and start again.'

'Have faith John,' she said.

By evening everything was ready for the off, and Brenda made a scratch supper and we sat listening to music on a battery driven CD player as the sun set.

Eventually around nine I said. 'Come on, bed time. It's an early start in the morning.'

'One last drink,' said Ugly and he charged our glasses with the best brandy on the place, and as the sun settled into the sea we drank to each other before we retired for the night.

52

THE NEXT MORNING we were up before dawn, and on our way as the sun crept up over the trees to the east.

We followed the coast road at first, and although we saw no one I noticed that a lot more of it had been cleared of stalled vehicles than the last time I'd taken it. Obviously traffic was beginning to move again. Then we cut up to Tonbridge Wells, bypassing the town, and then on to Dartford.

It was a revelation. The roads around the town were totally clear. And as we arrived at the entrance to the tunnel I saw something I never thought I'd see again a traffic jam. Admittedly it was only two vehicles, a Suzuki jeep and a Transit van, but it made my stomach turn.

The two vehicles were queuing at the southern tunnel entrance which was guarded by four men dressed in a motley collection of combat gear, denim and leather, carrying a variety of weapons.

I stopped the Land Rover a hundred yards behind the Transit and saw the four men notice our arrival and bring their weapons up into firing positions. 'What do you say?' I said to no one in particular.

'We've come this far,' said Ugly.

I let the truck drift forward. 'Keep your weapons out of sight,' I said. 'We don't want any trouble.'

I drew up behind the Transit as the Suzuki moved into the tunnel itself and two of the men came round the van, one each side. The one on the right who I took to be the leader gestured for me to lower my window which I did.

'Morning,' he said.

'Good morning.'

'Not seen you before.'

'No.'

'Where you from?'

'The coast.'

I watched out of the corner of my eye as the other man bent and peered into the truck. The Transit drove off after a box had been handed over, and the other two men guarding the tunnel stood in front of the Land Rover.

'Where you going?' asked the leader.

'Essex.'

'Scavenging?'

I nodded.

'How did you know we were open?'

'We heard a radio station. Radio England.'

'All the way down there?'

I nodded again.

'That's good. If you heard them you know the deal. Got anything for us?'

'Sure,' I replied, got out of the vehicle, went to the back, opened the tailgate and showed him one of the boxes that Brenda had prepared.

He looked though it, brought out a bottle of vintage Burgundy and smiled. 'This is good stuff,' he said.

'So I'm told.'

'You're told right.'

'So can we go through?'

'Of course. Jackie.' He called one of the other men who was obviously reassured by his tone, shouldered his weapon and came to collect the box. Meanwhile the boss reached into one of the pockets of his combat trousers and came out with a battery driven radio. It occurred to me to wonder what would happen when all the available batteries had run out of juice, as he keyed in a number and said. 'Land Rover coming through. Taxes paid.' I heard another voice though static and the boss killed the radio. 'My name's Lenny,' he said and stuck out his hand. 'I'm in charge of this little lot. Will we see you again?'

'John,' I said and shook hands. 'On the way back in a few days.'

'Don't forget to have something for the lads at the other end,' he said.

'No problem.'

'On your way then and good hunting.'

'Cheers,' I said and went back to my seat, put the truck into gear and entered the tunnel.

'Easy,' said Ugly as we drove through the darkness. Whatever else was working the lights inside the tunnel weren't.

When we got to the other side another group of men waved us down. I stopped the truck and let down my window again. One of them came over to the truck. 'Howdo,' he said.

'Hello.'

'Day trip?'

'A bit longer.'

'Coming back through?'

'Yeah.'

'Good. The more the merrier. You'll need another tax.'

'Lenny said.'

'Good. See you then.'

'See you.'

And we were off.

After that it was just a short hop cross country before Loretta pointed to a spidery mass of towers on the horizon and she said, 'That's it.'

It took us two days in all to complete the journey. Without the tunnel I reckon it would've been more like five.

Ugly parked the Land Rover in a wooded hollow and I took Loretta and the binoculars up a slight incline until we had a clear view of the refinery below us sitting on the edge of the estuary.

It was like an armed camp, with various bodies working on the tanks and pumps and guards with guns at every exit and entrance. It was almost as if The Death hadn't occurred.

'It's a lot busier than when I came before,' she said.

'Life's getting back to normal,' I remarked. 'They're doing business down there, and not just with Marco I'll bet.'

'But what happens when the oil runs out this time? They're living a fantasy life.'

'Aren't we as well?' I said.

'You know that this is only prolonging the agony. If we survive this winter what about next? Eventually there's going to be no fossil fuel left in this country.'

She was no fool our Loretta. 'Then someone will come up with the bright idea of importing it,' I said. 'You can't keep the human race down. We're not going to go back to being farmers scratching a living from the land. If there's two people left alive they'll work out some way to make profit out of each other. It's human nature. You remember disaster movies before the Death? End of the world films?'

She nodded.

'They got it all wrong. In them people went back to wearing animal skins and hitting each other with clubs. It isn't going to be like that. We were all brought up with technology and we all want central heating and microwaves again. There might not be many of us left, but look at the Dartford tunnel. Someone cleared that and started charging to use it. We'll be bartering at first, but I bet you within five years money will be back. It stands to reason.'

'You're very optimistic. So where will you lot fit in? You're highwaymen.'

'I didn't say it was going to be easy, I just said it was going to happen.'

'I hope we live that long.'

'So do I. P   erhaps if we can survive this winter, when the spring comes we can change. Perhaps we'll all be born again, and we won't need to rob and kill to survive. And you're going to be an important part in the rebirth. Literally. If your baby is OK, then we know that the human race will go on. There'll be other pregnant women. Probably are now.'

'And if it isn't OK?'

'Why shouldn't it be? You and the father were both immune. The chances are the baby will be too. And maybe The Death has died off itself. I haven't seen a case for months. Nobody seems to be worried about it now.'

'I suppose.'

'And what was that crack about you lot? It's us lot now isn't it? You're going to stay, aren't you?'

'Just try getting rid of me.'

I smiled and held her close and kissed her. 'And you said I was optimistic. Well I am, and you've got everything to do with that. Until you came I was a dead man walking. You've saved my life.'

'So does that make us even? You saved mine once too, remember?'

'I don't know,' I replied. 'I don't know what that makes us.'

53

THERE WERE TANKERS inside the compound of the refinery, but not the ones that belonged to Marco, and Loretta didn't recognise any of his men from Cambridge. Various vehicles came during the days we watched, loaded up with petrol and left. 'Why don't we ambush one of them?' she asked. 'They don't seem to be so heavily guarded.'

'It's Marco's fuel I want,' I said. 'It's personal.'

On the first evening we were there I took Loretta out in the truck just before darkness fell, and she showed me the first part of the route the tankers would take back home to The Last Chance Saloon. I found just the spot for an ambush as the sun extinguished itself behind the horizon. 'We'll check this out when it's light,' I said. 'OK?'

'I just hope we don't run into Marco's boys on the way,' she said.

'This is not the only Land Rover driving around,' I said. 'Life's returning. I doubt if they'd even notice.'

The next morning I took Ugly and Brenda to look at the spot I'd found. It was a dip in the road just after a tight bend and just before another. The convoy was bound to slow and that's when we'd take them. 'But we mustn't hit the tankers,' I said. 'Otherwise they'll be redrawing maps of this road. If they ever get around to making maps again,' I added. 'And remember, we take them with as little gunfire as possible. I know it's going to be difficult but we've got to have that fuel.'

We lay up by the Land Rover for another two days, taking turns to spy on the complex, and it was noon of the third when Ugly, who was on watch came hustling down the hill. 'They're here,' he said. 'I'd recognise them anywhere.'

Loretta and I went back up with him and we saw the two tankers I'd last seen at the back of Marco's pub, a dirty Range Rover and six bikes lined up on the other side of the wire.

'How many?' I asked Ugly.

'Fourteen,' he replied.

I'd been spot on with my forecast.

'Perfect,' I said. Then to Loretta. 'When will they leave do you think?'

'Tomorrow morning probably, so that they can get back in one day.'

'So tomorrow we move,' I said.

We kept watch on the complex all night. I took the eleven 'til one in the morning shift. It was just like *Mad Max Two* down there. Behind the barbed wire, concrete, and metal barriers that guarded the refinery, people ran around like ants lit by the flames that gushed from some sort of exhaust pipes that pushed up from the earth. It all looked bloody dangerous to me, but that was their problem. Ours was separating Marco's thugs from the precious cargo they were loading into the two tankers.

When Pansy relieved me at one I went back to our camp but couldn't sleep and lay awake until the dawn arrived.

She came over to my sleeping bag at three. 'Nothing happening much,' she said. 'Sandy's up there now.'

'Fair enough,' I said. 'Let's get some breakfast and get ready to move.'

We roused the rest of the camp and boiled water for coffee, but no one was in the mood to eat.

Ugly went up to our lookout and half an hour later he was back. 'Looks like they're getting ready to roll,' he said.

We'd packed up our gear whilst he was gone and I said. 'OK. Go get Sandy and let's split.'

We drove down to the ambush spot. The roads were deserted and I put Gwen into the top window of a house that overlooked the road the convoy would take. She could see for a mile or so across the flat landscape from there, and we could see the window from where we hid the truck. At her signal we'd put our plan into operation.

It was as simple as I could make it: According to Loretta the convoy was led by a flying 'V' of three bikes, then the Rover, then the two tankers and the rest of the bikes bringing up the rear, and Ugly confirmed that that was the configuration when they arrived.

I put Brenda and Sandy at the brow of the hill that the road took, just as it bent off to the right, one on each side, armed with shotguns. Ugly was in the Land Rover parked at the bottom of a track half way up the hill. He had the Uzi. His job was to cut off the Rover and the bikes at the front from the tankers and let Brenda and Sandy take care of them, then deal with the first tanker. Loretta was at the bottom of the hill with a rifle, and Gwen, armed with another shotgun, would join her when she'd spotted the convoy and signalled to us. Those two were to take care of the bikers in the rear. I posted myself halfway up the hill with the H&K and my Glocks. Opposite me was Pansy with her .30-30. Our job was to take out the driver and mate of the second tanker.

It was either going to work or it wasn't. Best case scenario: We ended up with the fuel. Worst case: The whole lot went up with a bang and everyone was dead.

Some choice.

54

WE TOOK UP OUR POSITIONS and waited. Only one vehicle went past in all that time, a big American 4x4 pickup that I imagined had been liberated as much for its monstrous looks as its cross country potential.

Ugly was sitting on top of the Land Rover with Puppy so that he could see Gwen's position more easily, and around eight I heard him shout. 'They're coming.'

I saw him scramble down off the truck, lift Puppy off the roof and drop her into the passenger seat. I hoped my dog would be alright.

Then Ugly started the motor just as I heard the first sound of powerful engines in the distance.

Shit, I thought. Here goes nothing.

The engine noises got louder. The deep rumble of the bikes, and the higher, yet equally as powerful sound of the diesels that drove the tankers. It crossed my mind that Marco must have a diesel supply too.

First the bikes rounded the corner to my right, slightly above me. They swept down into the dip, changing down through the gears, then started up the slight hill past me to where Brenda and Sandy were waiting. The bikes were polished and flashed reflections of the sunlight as they came. I saw rifles or shotguns in scabbards by the back wheels of the bikes, the riders were wearing handguns in holsters around their waists and I hoped that we hadn't bitten off more than we could chew.

Still they weren't expecting anything. This must be a milk run for them now after so long. Surprise was our only advantage.

The three bikes went past me closely followed by the Range Rover and the trucks dropped behind as they negotiated the narrow bends just as I'd hoped they would.

When the Range Rover passed the entrance to the track where Ugly was waiting, he put the Land Rover into gear and shot broadside across the tarmac in front of the first truck that had just passed me.

I heard gunfire from where Brenda and Sandy were waiting. A barrage of shots from their pumps that were almost too close together to count.

The second tanker's driver jammed on his brakes to avoid ramming the back of the first, and the cab nose dived exactly where I was crouching in the ditch. I jumped up, ran out into the road, leapt up onto the passenger's step, tried the handle of the passenger door and miraculously it opened saving me having to shoot through the glass. I jabbed the Glock inside into the surprised faces of the driver and his mate as the truck slid to a halt.

I heard shouts from behind the truck, and a load of shots from there too and I said. 'Knock, knock. You should've locked the door mate. Now keep your hands where I can see them.'

55

I PUSHED THE BARREL of the Glock into the passenger's neck and said to the driver. 'Into neutral, handbrake on, switch off. Give me the keys and you'll both live.' I didn't mention the alternative.

He did as he was told without a murmur. He was shocked and I wanted everything boxed off here at least, before he recovered.

From outside I could still hear sporadic firing as Pansy appeared at the driver's door and yanked it open. Her job had been to keep a bead on the driver and let him have it if he did anything drastic.

When the keys were in my jacket pocket, Sandy took a set of handcuffs from her belt and cuffed the driver to the wheel whilst I covered him and his mate, then she did the same to the passenger himself.

I tested that the handbrake was on fast and shoved the gear stick into the first notch I could find. I didn't want the truck rolling back. 'If either of you touch anything we'll know and we'll shoot you,' I said to them both. 'Just sit still,' and I turned and dropped out into the road and swung the H&K into firing position as Pansy joined me by the blunt nose of the tanker. I could still hear shooting from both up the hill and down it.

We ran up to the cab of the first truck. Ugly was covering the two inside with the Uzi through the open passenger door. Pansy and I repeated what we'd done in the other tanker securing the driver and passenger tightly. I gave them the same warning.

'You two go up, I'll go down,' I said to my companions when everything was secure.

Ugly didn't say a word, just took off with Pansy to where Brenda and Sandy had launched their ambush, and I headed down the incline to find Loretta and Gwen, my heart in my mouth.

When I got to the rear of the second tanker I saw three bikes lying in the road their engines still running. On the ground were the still bodies of two of the riders. The other was in the ditch on my side of the road shooting at Gwen and Loretta. At least I hoped they were both still alive. In fact I prayed they were even after what I'd said about God.

'Oi,' I said as I stepped out from the great tank that towered above me and that with one bullet could turn into a molten, liquid hell that would confirm or deny my knowledge of whether or not there was a God in a second, as it sucked me into its vortex.

The biker in the ditch looked up as if he expected me to be one of his pals bringing reinforcements, and when he saw that I wasn't his mouth formed a bristly 'O' and he began to turn his pistol in my direction, as I eased back on the trigger of the machine gun and stitched a bloody line across his torso.

The biker fell back and I legged it over the road to where Gwen and Loretta had been dug in. 'Gwen, Loretta,' I called as I ran. 'Are you alright?' Although to my shame it was really Loretta I was most worried about.

They came out of the ditch covered in leaves and dirt clutching their weapons and with no sign of injury. 'Thank God,' I said and gathered them both up in a hug.

Then I heard continued firing from the front of the convoy. 'Come on,' I said, 'the others are in trouble.'

With only a moment to check for life signs on the fallen bikers, of which there were none, the three of us ran up the length of the petrol train.

When we got to the Land Rover that was still blocking the road I saw Pansy kneeling behind the front wing sighting down the length of her rifle. We dropped down beside her and she gave us a tight grin. I hunkered up and peered through the glass of the cab and the Range Rover that had passed me was a shot out wreck sitting on four flat tyres slewed across the road. The windscreen and the glass all round had been destroyed, and there was no sign of life inside. The bikes had been dropped where they'd come to a halt, and the body of one of the bikers was half in and half out of the ditch. But at least two of the guards had survived and were in the ditch themselves keeping my troops pinned down.

'We're here,' I shouted at Ugly and he turned and grinned and beckoned.

'Cover me,' I shouted to the girls, and they laid down a barrage of shots as I zigzagged to where Ugly was waiting.

'Alright?' he said.

'Fine. No casualties. What about you?'

'Fine as far as I can see. We just need to get rid of this lot. How many of them are there?'

'Just two.'

'This'll do it,' I said, unclipped a grenade from my belt, pulled out the pin, turned towards the girls behind the Land Rover, put up my hand and waited until they stopped shooting, came up from the crouch I was in, let go of the spring and sailed the grenade into the ditch. I just had time to duck before it went off, and earth and muck rained down on the Range Rover and Ugly and me.

We waited for a few seconds. All was quiet except for the ringing in my ears and I ventured a look. There was no fire from the ditch and I ran out from behind the car and looked down into it. Two men were lying at the bottom, their clothes torn and covered in blood.

The convoy was ours.

56

AND WITH ONLY ONE CASUALTY.

When the shooting and the explosions stopped we all congregated at the top of the hill. Sandy's shirt was red with blood and Ugly went to her. 'Are you alright?' he asked with concern.

'Just a flesh wound,' she said.

'Let's have a look,' I said and she gingerly unbuttoned her shirt and there was a bloody crease along her side under her left breast. 'Get the first aid box Gwen,' I ordered. 'We can't afford for this to get infected.'

Gwen trotted off to our Land Rover and when she opened the door Puppy jumped out and came running to me, her ears back in fear. 'You're alright baby,' I said, squatting down and holding the frightened dog. I could feel her shivering in my arms and I must admit I was shaking myself.

Whilst Gwen was dealing with Sandy's wound, and Brenda found her a clean sweatshirt, the rest of us took a look at our prizes. There seemed to be no damage to the tankers, and Ugly used our Land Rover, which was peppered with bullet holes from the battle at the top of the hill, to push the wrecked Range Rover with its four dead occupants off the road.

I saw Pansy hunkered down over one of the bikes that had fallen at the front of the convoy. It was a handsome Harley-Davidson painted electric blue. 'Fancy it?' I said.

She nodded. 'Always wanted one.'

'Then we'll take it with us.'

She smiled.

Next we pushed the other five bikes into the closest ditches and with some difficulty, being as it seemed to weigh half a ton, hoisted Pansy's prize onto the back of the second tanker and lashed it there with rope.

The dead bodies of the biker outriders joined their machines, and all their weapons and ammunition went to strengthen our armoury.

That only left the two tanker drivers and their mates who were still cuffed to the steering wheels of the two vehicles.

We unlocked them and let them out onto the road where they bunched together rubbing the circulation back into their hands.

'What'll we do with them boss?' asked Ugly.

I knew what I should do. Make the four of them kneel by the side of the road and put a nine millimetre bullet through the back of each of their heads, standing slightly to one side to avoid any blowback of blood and tissue, but fate intervened.

The driver of the second truck, a tall, blond-haired man in his mid twenties was looking at us and he cocked his head and said. 'Loretta? Is that you?'

Loretta blushed.

'You know this bloke?' I asked.

She nodded. 'He was a friend of Mike's.' She'd told me that Mike was the father of her child.

'What are you doing here?' asked the driver, then he looked more closely at me and Ugly. 'I know you too,' he said. 'You were at Marco's. You killed our people. You pieces of shit.' And he lunged at us and Ugly chopped him in the head and he went down on one knee. He looked up at Loretta and said, 'Did you plan this you bitch?'

She said nothing in reply.

'So what are you going to do with us?' asked the driver, but he could see it in my eyes. 'Kill us in cold blood, is that it?' he said.

'You lot can talk about cold blood,' I said back. 'You had her whoring for you and you killed her boyfriend.'

'Not me,' said the driver. 'That was Marco.'

'And he was supposed to be your friend,' I went on. 'You deserve to die.'

Loretta looked at me with wide eyes. 'No,' she said. 'There's been enough killing.'

'They know who we are,' I said. 'I have to.'

'John please. Let them go.'

'What? Back to Marco? He's going to come looking for us.'

'He won't find us,' she pleaded. 'You can't just kill them.'

'I can,' I said.

'Then kill me too,' she said.

'Don't be stupid.'

'I'm not.'

I gestured at the other bodies in the ditches. 'You helped kill them.'

'That was different. That was survival. This is murder. If you do it we're finished.'

'Don't say that,' I said.

'I mean it.'

I looked at the others. 'What do you lot say?' I asked.

They shuffled their feet and looked at each other but no one spoke.

'If we let them live we're putting ourselves in harm's way,' I said.

Finally Ugly cleared his throat. 'I'm willing to take the chance,' he said.

The rest nodded.

'You're crazy,' I said, then looked at Loretta. 'Looks like you win.'

57

SO FOR THE SECOND TIME in days I allowed my heart to soften. The first time had been when I'd rescued Loretta from Marco and then allowed her into my bed and after that I knew that I could refuse her nothing.

So I let them go.

And in doing so, and allowing my feelings to stop me doing what I knew I should do, however terrible it would be to do it, I allowed a dreadful retribution to come down on us all.

When we were ready to leave we handcuffed the four of them again and pointed them back the way they'd come and let them walk. None of them spoke as we did it.

I watched as they went round the bend at the top of the first slight incline in the road, and the blond driver turned and looked back at me with such hatred in his eyes that I knew I'd made a terrible mistake allowing him to live, but by then it was too late. I knew that we would meet again sometime in the future and that if he could he would kill me as I should have killed him, with no compunction, like swatting a fly.

We climbed into the three vehicles, Brenda driving the Land Rover with Gwen and Patsy as passengers, Ugly at the wheel of the first tanker with Sandy by his side, and me driving the second with Loretta and Puppy for company.

With a crash of gears and a lurch from the big, heavy vehicle I took off in the wake of the others, and Loretta put her hand over mine on the wheel. 'You won't regret it,' she said. 'I promise.'

'I hope you're right,' I replied. 'And I hope that Marco never finds us, because if he does he won't be so merciful.'

She touched her stomach. 'He won't,' she said. 'I'm going to have a beautiful baby and the three of us will live happily ever after.'

'Just like in the story books,' I said.

She nodded happily. 'That's right. Just like in the story books.'

But then some story books were written by the Brothers Grimm.

We headed back the way we'd come. It took longer because of the size of the tankers and the fact we couldn't go off road with them. But eventually after a day and a half's drive we got back to Dartford.

The four men guarding the north side of the tunnel's entrance flagged us down. I got out of the rear tanker and walked to where one of the guards was talking to Brenda through the driver's window of the Land Rover. 'Is there a problem?' I asked when I got to it.

'No problem mate,' said the guard keeping his gun barrel hovering between Brenda and me.

'He wants petrol,' said Brenda.

'No,' I said. 'We've got a box of stuff in the back for you. Food and wine. Just like when we came through the other day.'

'I remember,' said the guard. 'But then there was only the truck and passengers. These tankers are full are they?'

I nodded. Shit, I thought, I should've known. The two bowsers full of fuel were literally worth their weight in gold. More. It was like winning the lottery pre-The Death and I'd been a bloody fool to let us come back this way.

'Is it petrol or diesel?' asked the guard.

'Petrol,' I told him. I didn't have much choice. It would only take a second to check.

'So we take a percentage,' said the guard.

'How much?' I asked.

'Half. You leave one of the trucks with us and the rest of you go on your way.'

'No,' I said. 'It cost too much to get them.'

'Then we'll take the fucking lot,' he said, swung the gun round on me and shouted to his mates. 'Watch 'em!'

Ugly made to get out of the first tanker and one of the guards fired into the air. 'Stay where you are,' he shouted.

'Be careful,' I said. 'That lot could go up.'

'I don't think so,' said the first guard. 'Now tell your people to get out and let's see their hands empty.'

'OK,' I said. 'Just take it easy.'

'We're are taking it easy,' he replied. 'Easiest take we've ever done.'

But he was wrong. He hadn't taken Loretta into account. In fact none of us had. She'd been leaning out of the passenger window of our lorry listening to what was going on, and suddenly she opened the door and swung out, the H&K I'd left in the cab in her hand, stuck it up against the skin of the tanker's bowser and yelled. 'You lot, drop your weapons or I shoot.'

The guard looked amazed. 'Leave it out, lady,' he said. 'If you do that we all die.'

'Then God'll sort us out you fucker,' said Loretta, and let loose a volley of shots that ricocheted off the tanker's chassis in a shower of sparks. Even I got a little jumpy at that. 'Next time it's straight into the tank,' she screamed. 'Now drop your guns.'

'I think she means it,' I said nervously and I wasn't putting it on. 'Are you willing to risk it?'

The guard licked his lips and let the barrel of his rifle drop, and I picked it out of his hand and the doors of our vehicles opened and everyone piled out and disarmed the rest of the guards.

'You greedy fucker,' I said to the head guard. 'People like you never learn,' and I slammed him in the stomach with the butt of his own rifle and he fell to the ground vomiting his breakfast as he went.

I grabbed him by the lapel and demanded 'Where's that radio?'

'Pocket,' he coughed, and wiped his mouth with his hand as I took the transmitter he used to communicate with his mates at the far end of the tunnel off him, smashed it onto the road and stamped on it until its case shattered.

'Cuff these fuckers,' I ordered, and within a few seconds it was done. 'Come on then,' I said. 'Let's get going, and stop for nothing at the other end.'

Everyone scrambled back into their various vehicles and we

took off at speed. At the other end of the tunnel we were though before the guards had time to register what was happening, and I breathed a sigh of relief as we left the exit behind. 'Christ,' I said 'That was close. You were great Loretta, you really saved the day. I didn't think you had it in you, especially after you made me let those four go the other day.'

'That was different John, I told you. A fight's one thing but cold blooded murder is entirely different. And I was peeing myself,' she said. 'Especially when I pulled the trigger. I thought the whole lot was going to go up with a bang.'

'You weren't the only one. Just one thing though.'

'What?'

'Would you really have blown us all up?'

She looked at me and smiled an enigmatic smile. 'You'll never know, will you John?'

And with that she refused to say any more.

58

IN THE WEEKS THAT PASSED after we got back to the house safely with our precious cargo, we were lucky enough to experience a glorious Indian summer that allowed us to get the house ready for the winter, and for me and Loretta to get to know each other properly. She was really showing her pregnancy by then, and we'd walk hand in hand along the cliffs and watch the sea dashing itself against the chalk below us. I worried about the things we'd got used to for expectant mothers in the latter years of the twentieth century. Things like scans and checks for all the sorts of problems that new babies have. But all those were gone. With this baby it was back to the old ways. Drop the child and go back to work in the fields. That sort of birth. I teased Loretta about it, but deep down inside I knew that all of us were worried that the baby would be all right.

We'd heard tell that there was a doctor living on the other side of Lewes, but although I took many a trip over there to find him, I never did. Brenda consoled me by telling me that the birth would be a piece of cake, and I just had to believe her. I had no other choice.

No other choice but to wait and to see that we would be comfortable when the bad weather came, as we knew it must.

Ugly scouted around and found spares for the generator which chugged away happily now we had plenty of fuel, giving us electricity throughout the house. The girls went hunting and filled two huge chest freezers with fresh meat whilst Ugly and I scavenged the neighbourhood collecting anything we could find. And we found plenty. Canned and bottled food of every variety. Not just staples like baked beans and tinned spaghetti, but all sorts of exotica that the good housewives of East Sussex had stashed away for special treats. Caviar; *foi gras; consommé;* lobster *bisque;* peaches in brandy. All sorts. But our best find was in an old stately home where the owner had been a wine and spirit freak. He must've had ten thousand bottles in his cellar and over two days we transferred them to the house.

We made trips to a couple of large out of town shopping malls which although they'd been stripped of food and drink still supplied everything else we needed to alleviate any chance of cabin fever over the dark months.

Each room in the house ended up with a large screen TV with stereo surround sound via a state of the art CD stereo system, a stereo VCR and DVD and a PlayStation. We collected thousands of CD's, videos, video games and armfuls of books. We looted PC World for personal computers, printers and lap-tops and raided WH Smith & Sons for enough stationery for each of us to write our memoirs.

Ugly also discovered a motorised snow blower that he thought might come in handy and chains for the tyres of our cars which now included a police Range Rover like the one I'd always wanted, which we found parked neatly on a slip road near Brighton with all its extras like shovels and full first aid kit intact, fuelled up and ready to go. How it had got there I'll never know. I drove it back with all the blue lights flashing and Ugly fitted it with a C4 plastique booby trap like our Land Rover and I stashed it away under the lean-to next to the old cottage for emergencies.

Each day we took it in turns to gather and chop wood for the open fireplaces and the kitchen stove and Ugly even volunteered to clean the chimneys.

Ugly also talked about finding and fitting a water pump between the stream and the house when spring came. It would be a massive job, but would save us the daily chore of filling buckets and transferring the water to the tanks in the house.

We all knew that we were living off the cadaver of a dead society, but that was all we could do. Maybe by this time next year a new society would be born.

So, when autumn arrived we were as ready as we were ever going to be for whatever was to come.

And of Marco there was still no sign.

59

WHEN THE WINTER DID COME, it came early and it came hard.

The first snow arrived in mid-November. The night before it was cold and the moon was bright when we all went to bed. Loretta and I watched a film on video whilst Puppy snored delicately from her position at the bottom of the bed. It was a comedy about a domestic situation, but I watched the background. Cars, people, the New York skyline. Something that had been so normal just a year before but now was as alien as the surface of the moon. I wondered what New York was like that November night. I wondered what horror stalked those dark skyscrapers now.

When I awoke at eight by my watch there was a strange luminous light in the room. I rolled out of bed, pulled on my blue jeans and went to the window. Outside, although the sun hadn't risen, was a sea of white. There must've been six inches of snow on the ground and more was falling in great white flakes.

I cleaned my teeth and woke Loretta.

'What?' she complained sleepily.

'Come see,' I said.

She got out of bed, pulled on her robe and came to the window. 'God, John,' she said. 'Where did that lot come from?'

'Up in the sky,' I replied.

'It's beautiful.'

'Maybe.'

'Do you think it'll stay?'

I looked up at what I could see of the sky through the veil of white. Dawn was just breaking and the clouds were iron grey and very low. 'It looks like it could last for months,' I replied.

'But we'll be alright.'

'Course we will. We've got everything we need for a long siege. The rest of the winter if needs be.'

'And we've got each other.'

I leant down and kissed her. 'That too,' I said.

'You're not regretting it. Taking me in,' she patted her stomach. 'And whatever this is.'

'Not a bit,' I replied. And I meant it.

'Well, let's go down and take a walk. I want to feel the snow on me. And Puppy will love it. We'll build a snowman.'

'Whatever you want sweetheart,' I said. And I meant it.

Nobody else was up when we got downstairs. The others had got into the habit of sleeping fairly late, but Loretta's pregnancy had made her restless and we were always first to rise. There was nothing much else to do. Loretta and I made coffee, then stood in the kitchen and put on the Wellington boots and heavy coats we'd liberated on our travels. Mine was leather lined with sheepskin, hers a ranch mink that had had a ten thousand pound price tag on it in the store where we'd found it. Now was no time for animal liberation. Jesus. The animals were that liberated they'd probably end up taking over the planet.

The kitchen was cosy and warm from the electric heaters we left on all night and I said. 'You sure about this?'

'Of course, I've always loved the snow. Ever since I was a kid.'

'It'll be cold out there.'

'In this?' she stepped back and gave me a twirl. 'You're joking. I'll be like a bug in a rug.'

'OK,' I said. 'Just watch yourself.'

I opened the back door of the house and stepped out onto the porch. It was freezing outside, feeling like it had dropped ten degrees in temperature during the night, and the snow was still pouring down. Puppy looked up into the sky as if the snow was a personal affront to her. 'Go on,' I said and shoved her down the steps into a drift where she floundered like a beached whale. She yipped, caught a flake of snow on her nose and licked it off. She seemed to grin and set off through the snow leaving a trail behind her.

I grabbed Loretta by the hand and gingerly we went down the steps ourselves. 'Be careful,' I said. 'Any broken bones we'll have to set ourselves.'

'I will,' she replied and we walked through the world of white in Puppy's wake.

It was deadly silent except for our noise and the soft rustle as the snow settled. When Puppy was out of sight and earshot I stopped Loretta by catching at the sleeve of her coat and said. 'Hold your breath.'

'What?'

'Just do it.'

We both did and the silence was so loud it filled my ears as if I was listening to white noise through headphones.

'I've never known such silence,' she said.

'I hope it's like this 'til spring,' I said. 'So that no one can get in or out.'

She held me tight and her nose and chin were cold against my face and we just stood hugging until the coating of snow would have made us look like one great person.

60

WHEN WE BROKE THE HUG and I looked round towards the house, I saw Ugly's grinning face from inside the kitchen window and I beckoned. Within seconds he was outside on the porch. 'Come on,' I shouted. 'The water's lovely.'

He reached inside the door and brought out his own coat and slipped it on, then he said something to someone inside and one by one Brenda, Gwen, Sandy and Pansy joined him wearing a selection of winter clothes. They all picked their way down the steps into the snow. Loretta and I walked back and joined them.

'It's incredible,' said Pansy, hoisting her rifle onto her back by its sling, then bending, gathered a handful of snow into a ball and lobbing it at Ugly's head. It struck him on the forehead, broke and cascaded down his face, flakes sticking in his beard like messily eaten ice cream.

'You cow,' he shouted, and made a ball of his own which he flung at Pansy's now retreating back, and almost before we knew it we were all engaged in a snowball fight like a bunch of twelve year olds. Even Puppy got into the act, returning from where she'd been to make her morning toilet covered in snow to her eye lashes and jumping up at everyone until eventually we all looked like walking snowmen and we collapsed into giggles and had to hold each other up.

When the excitement had worn off we went back inside, laid out damp our clothes to dry and all helped to cook a massive breakfast.

Afterwards we held an impromptu conference as the snow continued to pour down outside and coat everything with a blanket of white until it was almost unrecognisable.

'I've got as feeling this is going to last,' I said. 'We've been having some very strange winters for the last few years. Wet and mild without much snowfall and we're due a bad one. Of course I could be wrong, it could all melt by tomorrow morning but I doubt it. Our only problem as far as I can see is if the stream gets bunged up with ice and we lose our water supply. We're going to have to keep an eye on it. Otherwise I count it as a good omen. If Marco is still looking for his petrol and this snow is widespread he's going to be buggered. As far as I'm concerned this can last forever. Ugly. You're going to have to make sure that the tankers' pumps don't freeze up and that the generator keeps going and the Land Rover is AOK. The rest of us, well, we can take a holiday. There's plenty of food and booze and things to keep us occupied. Brenda's drawn up a rota for cooking and cleaning and if we keep our cool we can settle down for a pleasant winter together.'

'When's Christmas?' asked Gwen. 'We need a tree.'

'About seven weeks time by my reckoning,' I said. 'And there's a little growth of pines about half a mile away. Don't worry you're not going to miss out. I managed to find some lights and decorations the last time we went to the mall. It's all organised.'

'How long after Christmas is the baby due?' asked Sandy.

I looked at Loretta. We'd been keeping as accurate a calendar as we could. 'The middle of January,' she replied.

'Well we're as ready as we'll ever be for that happy event,' said Brenda. 'I've got books on it and as much gear as I could pick up to make it easy.'

'We'll be OK,' I said. Then smiled at Loretta. 'Don't worry love. It'll be a piece of cake just like Brenda says.'

61

AND, STRANGELY ENOUGH, both Brenda and I were proved to be right.

The snow did last. In fact the blizzard didn't stop for three days, and by then the drifts were twenty foot deep in parts and we had to dig trenches six foot deep to get to the tankers and the generator housing and the Land Rover, where Ugly, bless him kept all the engines and pumps working smoothly. Getting the snowblower had been a work of genius and saved us hours of hard labour. And it was fun using it. Creeping up on people and covering them with the spray of snow that fountained from the nozzle. Puppy especially loved getting in on the game. So much so that sometimes I had to dig her out before she suffocated.

After the first snow stopped it got progressively colder, well below zero during the days and the temperature plunged each night. But we were warm and snug in the house, and although the stream almost completely iced over, there was no time when there wasn't enough water for our needs.

After that it snowed on and off for months, with never a thaw between the falls. I took to walking Puppy once a day down to the where the track to the house joined the B-road at the bottom of the hill. Every day we stood, two black figures, one big and one little and looked at the unbroken white that covered the road, apart from some small animal tracks. And every day I thanked God that no one had found us. Not yet anyway, although deep down inside I knew something was coming. Something bad.

I made sure that Loretta got plenty of exercise, clearing a path towards the cliffs so that we could take a daily walk in that direction too. Or in her case, more like a daily waddle as the child grew bigger inside her.

Christmas came and went and Brenda and Gwen prepared a massive feast complete with crackers and paper hats, Christmas pudding with tinned custard and brandy butter, and when we turned off the lights in the dining room and opened the double doors into the sitting room where the tree was lit up I know that I wasn't the only one with tears in my eyes for people and things past.

People and things that could never return no matter how much we wished for them to do so.

Our first year after The Death ended with us all singing Auld Lang Syne and toasting each other with hundred year old brandy, but we were not to know that it would be the last New Year's that we would spend together ever.

62

LORETTA'S WATERS BROKE by our estimation at three forty-five on January the fifteenth 2001. Outside the snow was pouring down but inside we were as cosy as could be. We were in bed together with Puppy as usual patrolling the boundaries of the bedroom. Loretta nudged me awake and said. 'It's here.'

'What?' I mumbled.

'The baby. It's coming.'

'Are you sure?'

'Course I am.'

I was awake in a second, jumped out of bed and ran, wearing just a pair of boxer shorts to wake Brenda.

'Calm down,' she said as I hopped from foot to foot as she found her dressing gown. 'And turn your back. I'm not decent.'

'Jesus Bren,' I said 'This is no time for modesty.'

'Maybe not for you,' she replied, looking at my state of undress. 'But it is for some of us.'

I did as she told me to save time, and when she was dressed she followed me to our room. 'Get that bloody dog out of here,' she ordered as she marched in. 'And yourself too. Make yourself useful and get the kettle on.'

'For hot water for the delivery?' I said.

'No. For coffee. I'm parched. And get the other girls up. I may need some help here.'

I did as I was told again and pretty soon had roused the house.

Brenda told Ugly and me to stay out of the way, which we did. Him looking out of the kitchen window at the snow, me pacing the floor, chain smoking through my diminishing cigarette supply.

I remembered Dominique's labour with Louisa. Thirty-six long hours it had taken. Thirty-six hours of pushing and screaming and sweating which left my wife a shaken wreck.

But Loretta was different. Within what only seemed like a few minutes, but must in reality have been just over an hour, Brenda came down to the kitchen now dressed in day clothes and said,

'Congratulations. It's a boy.'

'Is it all over?' I said.

'Bar the shouting, or in his case screaming. He's got a healthy pair of lungs.'

'Is he alright?'

'Course he is. Loretta's a natural. Now where's those kitchen scales? I need to weigh him.'

'Can I see them?'

'A minute. We're getting the room and the pair of them cleaned up.'

She found the scales and took them with her leaving me even more nervous than before.

'For God's sake relax,' said Ugly. 'Everything's fine.'

'I won't believe that until he's been out in the air for a few days. He could be vulnerable to The Death you know.'

'Don't be so pessimistic.'

I could hardly contain myself until Brenda and the other girls returned all as pleased as Punch with themselves. 'Is he still alright?' I asked.

'Of course. Seven pounds, three ounces.'

'Is that good?'

'Go see for yourself. You're making me twitchy. But don't stay too long.'

I went up to our room and found Loretta sitting up looking no more tired than if she'd taken a brisk walk, holding her baby wrapped in a white shawl. 'That was quick,' was all I could think to say.

'Thanks,' she said. 'Congratulations might be in order.'

'Sorry,' I said, leaning over to kiss her. 'Congratulations.'

'Take a look at your son,' she said.

And although strictly he wasn't, my heart was filled with such pride as I looked down into his wrinkly little face that he might just as well have been. 'A boy,' I said. 'That's great. What shall we call him?' We'd never discussed names before. I think we'd been too scared to in case something went horribly wrong.

'I think Adam is appropriate, don't you?' said Loretta.

I felt a great grin spread across my face. 'Adam,' I repeated. 'The first boy. That's perfect.'

63

WHEN ADAM WAS THREE DAYS OLD he woke us up early, coughing fit to bust in the antique cot that sat next to our bed. Loretta woke first and when I came to she was kneeling next to it, a stricken look on her face. 'What is it?' I said.

'I don't know. He's sick.'

I joined her on the floor. Adam's nose was running, he was coughing again and he'd gone bright yellow. 'I'll get Brenda,' I said.

I roused Brenda and Gwen and they rushed to our room. 'What is it?' asked Loretta again, grief written all over her face.

'A bit of jaundice,' replied Brenda calmly picking up the crying child and hushing him with a whisper. 'Some babies get that.'

'But the other,' I pressed, hardly wanting to say it. 'It's The Death isn't it?'

'I keep telling you,' said Brenda. 'Adam's immune. It's a cold. Look at the weather and you won't wonder at it.'

Loretta shook her head. 'No,' she said firmly. 'It's the Death.'

Brenda put Adam back into his cot and gathered Loretta up in her arms. 'Loretta,' she said. 'Believe me. It's a cold.'

The crisis came that night. Adam was hot and sweaty and his nose was running like a tap, the hack in his cough was almost too much for any of us to bear and he was refusing Loretta's nipple. All seven adults wandered the house unable to rest. Brenda cooled him with cold flannel, constantly taking his temperature with the back of her hand as he lay crying in her arms.

At three in the morning we were all sitting in the living room when Brenda said. 'His nose has dried up.'

'What?' said Loretta, jumping from the chair where she was dozing. 'But he's crying so loudly.'

'I think he might be hungry,' said Brenda. 'Give it a try.'

Loretta undid her blouse and unselfconsciously offered Adam her breast. He attached himself as if he'd never let go again, and she smiled. 'You're right,' she said to Brenda.

'If he's hungry, he's better,' she said. 'And I'm knackered. I'm off to bed. You coming Gwen?'

Gwen nodded. 'Only wake me if the roof caves in,' said Brenda and she was gone.

By day five the yellow had softened on Adam's skin, his cold had almost gone, and he was sucking on Loretta's breast like a fiend as we sat in the warmth of the kitchen. 'I told you didn't I?' said Brenda from her position by the stove where she was busy baking bread. 'But you wouldn't listen.'

'I know,' I said. 'We were just so frightened.'

'We all were,' said Brenda.

'So you weren't sure?'

'Not one hundred percent,' she replied. 'Who could be? But I was pretty sure.'

'Anyway thanks for your confidence,' said Loretta. 'I don't know what we'd've done without you. And at the birth.'

'That was all your doing,' said Brenda. 'Like shucking peas. You'll probably have ten.'

'You'd better check with John,' said Loretta blushing.

'I don't mind,' I said.

'Then you'd better get going,' said Ugly. 'Before he gets too old for the job.'

64

THE NEXT FEW WEEKS were the happiest I'd known since The Death came. I think they were the happiest any of us living in that big house on the cliffs outside Lewes had known. We were warm and safe, and Loretta had produced a new life. We all looked forward with anticipation to the spring when we could share the good news with others, and maybe start to get the world back on its feet. It was a bold, optimistic notion, and we should have known that the fates looked unkindly on boldness and optimism in those days. We'd forgotten that God had forsaken us like experiments in a jar when the school-boy scientist had gone home for the night.

It was as if we were, finally, the very last people on the planet, and only once did anything occur to spoil that feeling.

Pansy had taken to long, solitary walks along the cliffs and through the woods with only her rifle and her thoughts for company.

Then one grey afternoon she came crashing through the kitchen door, her cheeks aflame from running. 'Did you hear it?' she demanded.

'What?' I asked, looking up from the book I was reading.

'The engine.'

'What engine?'

'It sounded like a plane.'

'When?'

'Just now.'

'Where?'

'Over the sea.'

I looked at her and shook my head. 'I didn't hear anything.'

She shook her head in exasperation and went to find the others to see if they'd heard anything. But the answers were always in the negative.

'I swear I heard it,' she said when we were all gathered together.

'You were imagining things,' said Brenda.

'I wasn't.'

'Did you see it?'

Pansy shook her head.

'Well then.'

Before a row started I stepped in. 'It's possible,' I said. 'Maybe someone's got something up in the air. In future when ever we're out we'll listen.'

'You think I'm barmy, don't you?' said Pansy before storming off to her room.

She never mentioned the sound again and no one ever heard it and eventually we forgot all about it. We were stupid and indolent and eventually we paid the price.

Meanwhile we still kept to the old calendar with its odd and even months and we marked off the days as the nights slowly lightened, and the dawns came earlier as the planet turned on its axis and the season began to change. As January turned to February, and February approached March the weather improved slowly. There was still thick snow on the ground, and on my daily walks with Puppy, the road at the end of the track was still unmarked by humanity.

But we could all see the light at the end of the tunnel.

And we were beginning to run low on certain items in the house.

Adam was growing daily and he needed clothes. We'd also neglected to get child seats to fit into the cars. I know, I sound like a suburban dad, but in my foolishness, I almost believed that I was.

So, one morning when the sky was blue and the first buds were visible on the trees in the orchid I decided to make a journey to the shopping mall some ten miles away to pick up what we needed.

I went on my own because I wanted to be alone. Although we'd made it through months without any serious fallings out between us, we all needed a break, and I took mine in the Land Rover with only Puppy for company. One by one the others asked to accompany me, but I refused them. I was being selfish and my selfishness left each of them to their particular fate.

And why I chose that particular day I'll never know. Destiny? Karma? Who knows? All I do know is that it was the day that happiness ended for me and I should have known better to think that it would last.

There was a joke before The Death came that when you saw a light in the tunnel it was another train coming to run you down.

How true that was I was soon to learn.

65

IT WAS EARLY when I left, Puppy sitting on the passenger seat next to me. I'd taken my Glock in its shoulder holster and a sawn off pump action Winchester in case I met any bad guys.

Little was I to know that it was not my day for meeting bad guys. That day was yet to come.

I slid and splashed the truck down the lane then turned into the virgin snow that was the road at the end. It was fun surfing through the snow that was beginning to melt under the rays of the sun, as the chains on the tyres kept me from skidding off the road as I let the back end slide out on the corners and snow sprayed from under the wheels. It felt like the first day of spring and I laughed and ruffled the pelt on Puppy's head and she seemed to laugh along with me.

The journey to the mall was uneventful. I could see from the tyre tracks in the slush that other people had been there before me but I didn't see a soul on the way there or on the return journey.

The mall itself had been pretty well looted over the winter, and inside its dark concrete and glass walls I knew that our civilisation had truly ended, and only the thought of Adam kept my spirits up as I walked through the echoing caverns of the shops. There'd been a number of bodies there the first time Ugly and I had visited the place. We'd left them where they lay, and no one else had thought to do anything with them, and animals had nibbled at them when they'd been fresh, and as they rotted the flesh ran through the material and formed a black stain on the fake marble floors of the mall as the bones became more visible until eventually that's all that would remain.

It seemed a fitting epitaph for our society.

As I'd surmised there hadn't been much call for baby items since The Death and I found nappies, car seats and baby clothes pretty easily in Mothercare. Of all the shops that day its stock was the most complete. I loaded what I'd taken onto a massive shopping trolley and went into the big supermarket that took up almost the whole ground floor, and stunk of rot, but there was absolutely nothing of any use.

I wheeled the trolley back to the truck that I'd brought as close as possible the gap where the main doors had once been, without driving over the glass from them that littered the ground. I didn't want a flat tyre.

I loaded the stuff into the back and lit a cigarette. I only had a couple of hundred left and I knew that pretty soon I'd have to give up again or start smoking the leaves off the trees.

It was the first day that really got warm that year and there were puddles forming on the tarmac that had once been the main parking area and was still littered with abandoned cars covered with a crust of snow, and a great sadness came over me, and I couldn't wait to see my friends, so I threw away the cigarette end, climbed into the driver's seat and headed home.

66

WHEN I'D LEFT THE FARM I'd driven the truck on the left hand side of the road like a good citizen of old. It's hard to shake off the habits of a lifetime and I'd noticed that everyone who did drive did the same unless the left hand side of the road was blocked.

So when I drove back there was only one set of tracks on the road. Those on the opposite side to where I was, and in front of me was only virgin snow. It still amazed me that no one had left the house in all those months. And that no one had tried to come in. But it was a comforting thought, and made me feel safe.

As the car splashed through the softening snow throwing a wake on either side I chatted to Puppy over the sound of the music from the cassette player. 'Soon be home,' I said. 'I'll bet they'll be pleased to see us.'

The trees on either side of the road were bare of leaves and stood out starkly against the blue sky which had turned almost white as the afternoon approached. There was not a breath of wind that day and the branches were as still as if frozen.

Then, just as I was about to turn off the B-road into the lane, on the horizon I saw the one thing we'd feared more than any other—Smoke. A black column rose through the still air, and I knew, I just knew that it was coming from the house.

Ugly had warned that if there was ever a fire at the house, without the pump from the stream we could lose everything.

'Jesus,' I said and smashed my foot down so hard on the accelerator that the heavy truck fishtailed and almost ended up in the ditch that was only visible because the snow dipped slightly on both sides of the road and again I was grateful for the chains. I regained control and then something strange happened. The pillar of smoke that had been so straight suddenly dissolved as if a high wind had sprung up, but the trees close to me did not move.

I wrinkled my brow in puzzlement and suddenly everything

was clear. From behind the tree line, slowly, like a bug launching itself into the air, rose a helicopter. I couldn't believe my eyes as I heard the roar of its engine above the scream of the Land Rover's.

So that's how they'd done it. That's how they'd got in without leaving tracks.

I skidded the truck to a halt and leaned out of the side window to get a better view of the chopper. It was an army machine, single rotored, decked out in khaki livery and I saw that both side doors were open and the barrels of a pair of machine guns came into view as it slowly hovered and spun in mid air.

Then I realised that the truck must be clearly visible, like a cockroach on a white handkerchief, black against the snow, and the copter suddenly stopped spinning and headed my way.

I grabbed Puppy by the collar, threw open the driver's door and dived out of the vehicle dragging her behind me. 'Go,' I yelled. 'Go Pup,' and I threw her bodily in front of me, kicked her up the backside and she shot off like a startled rabbit with a yip of surprise.

I was only a step behind as the sound of the chopper's engine got louder and I could almost hear the gunners screaming to turn the machine so that they could get a clear shot.

I tore through the drift that covered the ditch, threw myself over the fence and ran into the trees. But they were bare and when I looked round and up, I could see the helicopter which meant it could see me.

I ran through the knee high snow then I saw Puppy. She'd stopped by a tumble of fallen branches covered in snow. She was no fool, and I dived and slid under their protection, dragging her with me, as the first bullets ploughed into the earth around me.

With my arms round her neck I burrowed deeper into the slush of melting snow, earth and leaves until suddenly the ground dropped away into a gully and we both rolled downhill until we ended up hard against the base of an evergreen that gave us some protection from the sky.

Heavy, metal jacketed bullets were ripping through the undergrowth all round us as the helicopter circled above us, the down blast from its rotor throwing up debris and creating a windstorm that threatened to blow away our shelter and expose us to the gunners above.

Then the firing dyed down only to commence again, but this time the bullets were aimed at the Land Rover. It only took seconds for them to hit the fuel tank and the truck exploded with a roar and more smoke rose into the air only to be battered down by the chopper.

I'd left the shotgun in the car, but I still had my Glock and a spare clip and I drew the gun and pulled Puppy even closer. If they landed I was going to take as many of the occupants of the helicopter with me as I could.

But it didn't come down. After a few minutes more circling and firing down at random, the great bird rose and headed off north.

I lay with Puppy in my arms until the sound of the engine had gone, then I rose from my hiding place, filthy dirty and soaking wet, and headed home with my dog at my heel and my heart in my boots.

67

I RAN ALONG THE LANE slipping and sliding on the wet snow, following Puppy who bounded ahead, her tail wagging as if it were some sort of game, and all the time the columns of smoke seemed to get denser and blacker. When I skidded to a halt on the turnaround my worst fears were realised.

The first thing I saw was Ugly's body sprawled on the thin coating of ice that covered the gravel. His shirt was dark with blood and he was perfectly still.

The house was gutted, as was the generator housing and the cabanas for the swimming pool. The two tankers were burning and the other vehicles in the compound were smoking wrecks.

I walked to Ugly's body and felt for a pulse but there was none, and his skin was already cold.

I stood up and shouted. 'Anybody there?' but there was no reply and all I got was an echo for my pains.

I walked round the burning house and found Sandy and Gwen together in the back garden, their bodies riddled with bullets. They were dead also.

I saw the gleam of brass on the ground and found a .30-30 shell casing. There was another a yard or so further on. Then more, and I followed the trail. Pansy had made it as far as the cliffs, but she too was dead, her throat cut. There was no sign of her rifle.

I walked back to the house as the sun made its fast descent into the sea. Then, from somewhere I heard a baby's cry.

I ran towards the sound shouting, 'Loretta, Adam. Is that you?' And from the darkness of the forest a single figure emerged carrying a bundle. 'Brenda,' I said when I recognised her. 'Where's Loretta?'

She staggered as she came towards me and I saw the tracks of the tears on her face. She gave me Adam and slumped against a tree. 'Gone,' she said. 'They took her with them before they set light to the place.'

'But the baby,' I said. 'How…?'

'I took him for a walk to give Loretta a break. I wanted to show him the spring coming. They came out of nowhere in that helicopter.'

'I saw it,' I said. 'They tried to kill me too. They wrecked the truck. Who was it?' But I knew.

'I was unarmed,' said Brenda. 'Not even a kitchen knife. Stupid. I had to watch. A little man in a frock coat.'

'Marco,' I said.

She didn't pay me any attention. 'I just hid,' she said. 'I didn't think you were coming back. Loretta was screaming. It was horrible.' Then something struck her. 'Where's Gwen?' she sobbed.

'I'm sorry,' I said and hugged her with one arm whilst holding Adam in the other.

'Oh Jesus,' she cried, and that set the baby off, and then Puppy arrived and started to whine herself as if she suddenly had realised what had happened, and all four of us stood together in the gathering darkness stricken with our own particular grief.

68

IT WAS GETTING progressively colder as the short evening came and I was soaking wet and shivering from rolling about in the snow and Brenda wasn't in a much better state, and I knew that if we didn't do something soon we could all die of hypothermia during the long night ahead. 'Did they find the old cottage?' I asked, looking in its direction with a feeling of relief that there was no sign of fire or smoke from it.

'I don't know, I didn't think,' gasped Brenda.

'Let's go see.'

We fought our way through the still thick snow and foliage in that direction, and when it came into sight it was still in one piece. I'd never been so glad to see a building in my life. Its old thatch was coated in snow and it would have been almost invisible from the air.

Puppy ran ahead and scratched at the door and I caught her up and threw it open. Inside it was musty and damp but it was shelter.

I found an oil lamp and lit it, and immediately started to make a fire. The kindling was reluctant to light but eventually it did and when the flames were licking at the logs I went into the kitchen.

Thank God for forward thinking. Everything was as I'd left it the previous autumn. I filled the kettle from one of the huge plastic bottles of water and put it on the Calor gas stove to heat. Then I went upstairs and found dry clothes and changed.

I went back to where Brenda was sitting in shock on the sofa holding Adam to her breast. 'Go and get changed,' I said. 'There's dry clothes in the main bedroom upstairs.'

'They're all gone,' she said quietly.

For a moment I thought she meant the clothes, then I realised she was talking about our friends. 'Brenda,' I interrupted before she could sink further into a funk. 'We're alive. Adam's alive. We have food and shelter. We must think of ourselves.

It's a tragedy, but we've been through tragedies before. If we curl up we die. Understand?'

She looked up at me and nodded.

'Now go change,' I said. 'I'll make some tea and we can work out what to do next.'

'But they're out there,' she said. 'All alone.'

'We'll sort them out tomorrow,' I said. 'There's nothing we can do now. Please Brenda, snap out of it.'

She started to cry then and that set Adam off and I sat next to her and took her in my arms. 'We've got to be strong,' I said. 'Please. For Adam's sake if no one else's.'

She nodded and brushed her eyes with her wet sleeve. 'OK,' she said. 'I'm fine now. Where did you say those clothes were?'

After a while Brenda stopped crying and became more like her old self and we started getting organised. I made hot, sweet tea for us and reconstituted some powdered milk for Adam. I knew it wasn't right as he'd been breast feeding but it was all we had. Brenda found dry clothes for herself and then had to change Adam's nappy. Of course that was one thing I hadn't made allowances for. Damn, I thought. All the stuff I'd got for the boy had been burnt up in the truck. Brenda adapted a napkin from a tea towel and then made scratch meal for us, mashing tinned vegetables for Adam.

When we'd eaten I aired the bedclothes in front of the fire and made a cot for Adam out of a drawer from the desk that sat in the living room, then made up a bed each for Brenda and me.

Doing the chores seemed to have taken her mind off the loss of our home and friends for a while but after we'd eaten she sat on the sofa cradling Adam and stared into the fire.

'Right,' I said. 'Loretta was alive when they took her, yeah?'

Brenda looked up and nodded.

'A sodding helicopter,' I said. 'I could hardly believe it.'

'How do you think I felt?'

'Yeah,' I said. 'Thank God you were away.'

'I might've been able to help.'

'Help yourself get killed,' I said. 'And maybe Adam too.'

'I think Loretta would've died herself before she let that happen. And you.'

I nodded. I was feeling more and more guilty about having gone on my expedition. 'I'm sorry Bren,' I said.

She looked startled. 'For what?'

'For not being there.'

'They would've killed you for sure. That little guy was furious about something. I was watching from the tree line. He was almost dancing when he spoke to Loretta. I'll bet it was because you'd gone. He kicked Ugly's body.'

'Bastard,' I said. 'I wonder where the hell he did get that helicopter and fuel. Maybe that was it. Maybe that's why he didn't land when they shot up the truck. Maybe they were worried about the fuel situation.'

'How do you think they found us?'

'It was my bloody silly fault. I told Marco that we had a place on the south coast the day we shot up his pub. After we stole the fuel his men probably talked to those people at the Dartford Tunnel. They'd be only too pleased to tell them about the tankers that broke through that day. Then remember Pansy thought she heard an engine one afternoon and we almost laughed in her face?'

Brenda nodded.

'Pansy thought it was a plane, didn't she? A pound to a penny it was a bloody helicopter. We never thought about camouflaging the tankers and that generator gave off a lot of exhaust. That bloody chopper was probably fitted with a heat seeking device. I bet they used it and maybe dropped someone off to take a look see and that was that.'

'You mean we were spied on.'

'Maybe. Maybe not. But they certainly found us didn't they?'

She nodded sadly. 'Do you think they'll come back?'

I shrugged. 'Who knows?' I said. 'But I think we'd better be long gone.'

'Where?'

'Well don't know about you Brenda,' I said. 'But I'm going to go and find Loretta.'

'What about Adam?' she said.

'Those women down by the sea shore. We'll go see them. They'll look after him I'm sure. A couple of them lost babies in The Death. They'll take care of him. You can stay there too if you want.'

'And you're going after Marco?'

I nodded.

'On your own? He's got an army. We saw that yesterday.'

'Ugly and I took him on once and survived. And we got the petrol.'

'And look where that got us.'

'We weren't counting on an airborne attack.'

'He'll be expecting you.'

'Probably. Unless he thinks I was killed with the truck.'

'He'll be expecting you,' she repeated. 'That's why he took Loretta alive.'

'I imagine.'

'And you'd go on your own?'

'I've got Puppy.'

'Puppy can't handle a gun.'

'But she's company.'

'So am I.'

'You mean you want to come?'

'Try and keep me away.'

'Thanks Brenda,' I said. 'I hoped you'd say that.'

'They killed Gwen. And the rest. We were like a family.'

'We were that. I thought we might be able to change our ways. Live in peace. But he wouldn't let us.'

'Maybe we weren't meant to. Live in peace I mean,' she said.

'Maybe not. Maybe we're all cursed to carry on killing until there's not a human being left on the planet.'

'I can't believe that, looking at him,' she said, gently touching Adam's sleeping head.

'Then maybe he'll do a better job than we did.'

She nodded her agreement, and yawned.

'We need to sleep,' I said. 'We've got a lot to do tomorrow.'

She agreed and I kissed her cheek, watched her walk upstairs, extinguished the lamps we'd lit, took Adam up to my room and put his cot beside me on the bed then lay down and tried to sleep.

I didn't have much joy.

69

FIRST THING THE NEXT MORNING after we'd fed Adam and managed a bite to eat ourselves, I checked the police Range Rover parked up under cover next to the cottage. Thank Christ it had been. If the chopper crew had seen it, they'd've blown it away too. That and the cottage with it and we'd probably all three have died the previous night. It started on the button, the chains were tight on the tyres, the twin tanks were topped up and there was a ten gallon can of petrol in the back. I blessed Ugly for his thoroughness and sitting in the driving seat with the engine warming up in the freezing morning air I cried for my friends for the first and only time.

Then we got round to the worst job. I drove Brenda with Adam in her arms back to the house. The fires had died down although there was still some warmth in the ashes despite the weather.

We found our friends' bodies and they were frozen solid as they'd died. We carried them to the front of the house and lay them together and it was one of the saddest sights I'd ever seen, their arms and legs sticking out at strange angles as if they were pointing at something we couldn't see. The Range Rover contained a pick and shovel and after we'd gathered the bodies together we tried to dig graves, but the ground was frozen solid too.

'What'll we do?' said Brenda with tears in her voice.

'We'll have to burn them,' I replied.

'Oh no.'

'It's the only thing to do Bren,' I said. 'Even if we manage to dig at all, the graves will be so shallow that animals will dig them up come spring.'

She was appalled at the thought. 'How will we burn them?' she asked.

'We're never coming back here, are we?'

'Never.'

'Then let's take them to the cottage and burn them inside it. It'll be fitting.'

She agreed, and we loaded the four bodies into the back of the police car and I drove them back to the cottage, vowing that once this was over I'd never touch the vehicle again either.

We took them into the living room and laid them on the floor.

The previous night I'd checked the weapons that Brenda had stashed in the cottage the previous summer in case of emergencies. They were still wrapped up in the sports bag we'd taken from Marco. There was an H&K MP5, an Uzi carbine, a Mossberg six shot pump action shotgun, a Colt .45 semi-automatic pistol, clips for the machine guns, ammo for all four guns and one hand grenade. I checked the weapons; their actions were smooth and oily. I loaded all the spare clips and finally found a length of twine and hung the hand grenade around my neck by its pin. If all else failed and I was brought down, at least with that secret weapon I could take a few of them with me. Then we took anything else useful from inside the cottage and loaded the truck, and when we were finished I emptied the contents of the paraffin lamps over the bodies of our dear friends.

We stepped back to the door and I said. 'Do you want to say anything?'

Brenda shook her head. 'You?' she asked.

'I think I should.'

There was an old illustrated Bible on the bookshelf and I turned to Revelations Seven. I'd read a lot of the Bible over the winter and the Book of Revelations seemed to say a lot about our current situation. Pestilence and famine and the wrath of God. There's a lot of horror in that book but I read out a milder passage:

'Therefore are they before the throne of God,
and serve him day and night within his temple;
and he who sits upon the throne will shelter them with his presence.
They shall hunger no more, neither thirst any more;
the sun shall not strike them, nor any scorching heat.
For the Lamb in the midst of the throne will be their shepherd,
and he will guide them to the springs of living water;
and God will wipe away every tear from their eyes.'

'That was beautiful,' said Brenda, and I lit a match and threw it into the room onto the paraffin. The flames danced across their bodies and I dragged her outside and we watched as the cottage caught light and burnt to the ground.

70

WE WERE SADDLED UP and off by noon, and the tall column of smoke from what was left of the cottage was in my rear view mirror all the way down the lane. In fact, every time I looked into it until eventually I finished with the truck, I could still see its ghostly reflection.

Ugly had loaded up this vehicle with plastique too and on the drive I explained to Brenda how to work it. She was going to be my Trojan horse. Marco and his mob had never seen her, so she was going to go to the Last Chance Saloon first and on her own.

'Those two drivers and their mates saw me,' she said.

'Only for a bit, and they were terrified I was going to shoot them,' I replied. 'And with Marco's idea of justice I doubt they survived when he found them. If he found them. Personally I'd've got as much distance between him and me as I could if I was one of them... But if you don't want to risk it.'

'Of course I want to risk it,' she said scornfully, more like the old Brenda I knew. 'I was just saying.'

'Fair enough. Do you remember what they looked like?'

'No.'

'There you are then.'

'OK John, you win.'

'Just be careful, that's all.'

She nodded.

We drove down the coast to where the women lived in their strange village of upside down boats, and Brenda took Adam in first. The women didn't really trust men that much.

Eventually she came out with their leader, an old hippie of maybe sixty years old dressed in a long skirt and an oilskin coat. 'Is that your baby?' she asked without preamble as she stuck her head in the driver's side window.

'Sort of,' I replied.

'It either is or it isn't.'

'It's a long story,' I said.

'Well whoever's he is, he's a miracle.'

'He is that.'

'Where's his mother?'

'Didn't Brenda tell you?'

'You tell me.' See what I mean about trusting men?

'Some people took her,' I said. 'They want me and they know I'll go to where she is.'

'Do you think you'll get her?'

I shrugged. 'I don't know.'

'What happened to your house?'

'It was burnt.'

'And the rest of you?'

I looked at Brenda. Hadn't she explained? But I answered nevertheless. 'They're all dead. All but Brenda and me and the child's mother.'

'And you want us to keep him?'

I nodded.

'For how long?'

'How do I know?' I said. 'Maybe we'll find his mother, maybe we won't. Maybe we'll be killed and maybe we'll survive. Maybe we'll come back and maybe you'll never see any of us again. It could be a week, it could be forever.'

'And the child was conceived after The Death?'

'That's right,' I said. 'Look at him. He's only a few weeks old.'

The woman nodded. 'These people,' she said. 'The ones that killed your friends and burnt your house. Do they want the baby?'

'I don't even know if they know about him. And I can't see any of them being exactly maternal or fraternal.' I shook my head. 'I don't think so.'

'But a baby could be a valuable item. In these times of trouble and misery.'

I put my head down on the steering wheel. 'Listen,' I said. 'If you don't want to care for him that's fine. We'll find someone else.'

'I didn't say that,' she said. 'I just wanted to know. Of course we'll look after him.'

I breathed a sigh of relief. 'We don't have anything for him,' I said. 'Nappies, baby food. They were all destroyed.'

She brushed me off with a movement of her hand. 'We don't care. It'll be a labour of love to adapt things for him. His name's Adam, right?'

I nodded again.

'A fine name. And his mother, if she should ever return without you?'

'Loretta,' I told her. 'She's small, dark and pretty.'

'I suppose she would be.'

'And you'll bring him up if we don't come back?'

'Just try and stop us,' she said. 'Ruth and Rosemary both lost their youngsters to The Death. They're inside, just as pleased as punch to be holding a little one again.'

'But if we do survive we'll want him back,' I explained.

'And you'll have him. But let's not talk of that now. Do you want to come in and say goodbye?'

I shook my head. 'No,' I said. 'We need to get on. The sooner we get there the sooner we get back. And the people who've got his mother. They may hurt her. They're not the kindest people on the planet.'

'And you are?'

I shook my head yet again. 'No,' I said. 'That's why we're going.'

We left the woman and went back to the truck. Overnight the wind had changed and was coming from the north again. It looked like the weather was changing for the worse.

It suited my mood perfectly.

WE DROVE STRAIGHT from the coast to Cambridge with only a stop to grab a few hours sleep when the night was at its blackest.

I retraced the route that Loretta, Ugly, Puppy and I had driven on those long hot days last summer. It was almost as if the summer had never existed, so cold and bleak was the weather and the countryside we drove though. On the way we saw the occasional vehicle but no one interfered with us and my Glock stayed safe in its holster.

After some to-ing and fro-ing I eventually found the field with the gates I'd smashed down whilst we'd been making our escape, and around one-thirty in the afternoon of the second day on the road, I pulled the Range Rover into the little lane where Ugly and I had parked on our last visit, and Brenda and I got out of the truck. 'Just a little stroll to get the lay of the land,' I said.

We left Puppy inside the warmth of the cab and pushed through the hedge and hiked across the thick snow that cracked under our footsteps to the ridge that looked down onto the pub. 'That's the place,' I said.

The building sat under its coating of white with just the glow of the coloured light bulbs peeping through at intervals. The car park was a mess of filthy slush, there were several 4WD vehicles parked close to the front, and half a dozen bikes lined up like they'd been the last time. 'They never learn,' I said.

'What?' asked Brenda, her breath thick on the freezing afternoon air.

'Nothing,' I replied. 'It doesn't matter.'

There were now three tankers parked in the compound at the back, next to the earth moving machinery, and the generator was chugging along merrily. Marco had replenished his fuel supplies without much difficulty, and that made me burn inside even harder at the thought of what he'd done to our little settlement.

There was no question now that it had been him, because in the field beyond the compound, close to the river which seemed almost frozen over, the edges of the ice laced with snow, was parked the helicopter that had strafed my Land Rover after attacking the house and killing my friends.

Brenda spotted it too. 'Bastards,' she said.

We lay next to each other in the snow together for a few minutes passing the binoculars back and forth until she grunted. 'Seems easy enough.'

'It is,' I said back. 'They'll check you for weapons at the gate and let you through. Just tell them you fancy a hot toddy.'

'I'm sure that'll work,' she said.

'Why not?' I asked. 'It's a pub isn't it?'

We slid back through the snow until we could stand without being seen from below and trudged back to the truck. Brenda got into the driving seat and Puppy joined me on the track. In some places the snow was so deep she was almost submerged. I opened the bonnet of the truck and set the clock that armed the detonator attached to the plastique. 'Now you know what to do,' I said when the bonnet was down again. 'Park up as close to the pub as you can, switch off, turn on the ignition again, then switch it off. That arms the bomb. Then you've got exactly two hours. I'll be watching from the hill. Just make sure you know exactly what time by your watch it's going to blow. I'll synchronise when I see you leave the truck.'

She nodded affirmation as I took my weapons and ammo from the back of the truck. That left just the Colt .45 that we'd tucked up back behind the rear seat. It would take a real close search to find it and I didn't think the guards on the gatehouse were going to be that thorough.

'Then I'll join you later,' I said. 'I don't know exactly when. Just be ready. And don't forget to be nice to the boys.'

'Don't worry,' she replied with a bitter tone to her voice. 'They're going to love me.'

'I believe you Bren. Good luck and take it easy.'

She nodded again, put the truck into gear and drove off. I

checked the clip on the H&K, slung the Uzi up higher on my shoulder and set off with Puppy across the field again.

By the time we got back to the vantage point Brenda had stopped the Range Rover at the gatehouse. The guard listened to her story, searched the truck and Brenda, taking plenty of time making sure she had no weapons hidden in intimate places but missing the Colt because he was too busy copping a feel. I put the bins on her face as he was fumbling around under her jacket and I could tell by the look on it that she dearly wanted to break his neck. I smiled, and almost as if she could see me she smiled back. Don't worry, I thought. Our time is near. Eventually the guard was satisfied and Brenda got back into the truck and he waved her through. I breathed a sigh of relief as she parked between two cars and got out of the Range Rover after a few moments and went inside. I looked at my watch. It showed three o'clock.

The night comes fast at that time of year in the fen country, and within half an hour it was almost dark, the only illumination remaining coming from the lights on the roof reflecting off the snow. 'Come on Pup,' I said. 'Let's take a look around.'

We moved down the hill keeping close to the hedges as the wind whipped the top layer of snow around us until visibility was almost nil. But then, if I couldn't see them, they couldn't see me. Which was just the way I wanted it.

72

AS I PROWLED round the perimeter it started to snow again. Huge, creamy white flakes fell from the sky covering Puppy and my tracks as we walked. Puppy soon resembled a Husky and stopped to shake the snow from her coat. 'Come on girl,' I whispered. 'Not long now.'

When I'd completed the circuit I looked at my watch again. Less than one hour to go. And time for me to make an appearance.

In almost blizzard like conditions I approached the gate house from the side and squinted through the glass through the condensation on the inside. The guard was sitting hunched over a Calor gas heater. Obviously he wasn't expected any further visitors that evening. I went to the front and gently eased the door open. The influx of cold air hit the guard and he turned towards me. I showed him the pump I was carrying. Nothing concentrates the attention like a shotgun, I've discovered, and he froze. I covered my lips with one finger and said. 'Not a word.'

He just looked at me with saucer eyes and threw him the sports bag that I'd brought with me. 'Put all the guns in there.'

He stood up and did as he was told, and I took the bag back, now weighed down with metal and dropped it at my feet. 'Turn round,' I said. He did so and I smashed the butt of the shotgun onto his head and he dropped to the floor like a stone.

I grinned, picked up the bag, stepped outside and lobbed it into the middle of the river where it sank through the ice that covered the water.

I looked out over the car park. It was deserted and the fresh snow was covering the slush. 'Come on girl,' I said to Puppy. 'Time to make an entrance.'

I walked across the tarmac, up the steps and kicked open the doors. Inside it was warm and noisy and the juke box was on at full blast. Brenda was by the bar, a glass in her hand and a biker on each side vying for her attention.

I looked up and my blood ran cold. On one of the poles sticking out from the wall in front of me was Loretta's head. Her hair was matted and her eyes had gone up into their sockets so only the whites were visible.

That was it. That was when I knew that only Marco or I would walk away from the building tonight. One of us had to die, and frankly, right then I didn't care which one of us it was.

Nobody had taken notice of me as I entered so I lifted the barrel of the shotgun and shot shit out of the Wurlitzer.

Now that did focus their attention.

73

'EVERYBODY STAY STILL and let's see some empty hands,' I said, racking another shell into the shotgun's chamber and waving the smoke away that wreathed round my head.

Everyone in the room seemed stunned by my entrance except for Brenda who pulled out the Colt she'd had hidden in the Range Rover and stuck it into the face of the biker to her right. 'Not your type,' I said and took the Uzi off my shoulder and tossed it to her.

She caught it one handed, put the semi-automatic away, pulled back the lever on the machine pistol and prodded the biker in the stomach. 'Sit down fat boy,' she said. 'And stop breathing your stink into my face.'

So far, it had been just a walk in the park, but I knew that could and probably would change in a second. Who knew what number of concealed weapons were hidden away inside the pub and who knew who'd be stupid enough to be the first to go for one? We'd had the element of surprise on our side so far, but it was only a matter of time before that changed and someone took a chance. The odds were two to God knows how many, and sooner or later someone would be bright enough to work that out for themselves.

I made for the door to Marco's office handing Brenda a couple of loaded clips for the Uzi as I went. It was locked and I fired into the woodwork and blew the lock to hell and gone.

I kicked the door open and went into the office gun first. It was empty. Shit, I thought, turned and everything went off just as I knew it would eventually.

I heard the sound of a shot from the bar, spun round as Brenda opened fire with the Uzi. I stuck my head through the door and saw her spraying a table load of bikers with the gun knocking them to the floor in sprays of blood. Nice, I thought as I picked a target and blew a coil of intestines out of the stomach of a hairy bloke with a small pistol in his great big paw. So much for no firearms!

Brenda had jumped over behind the bar and was busy changing magazines as I stood in the doorway and emptied the Winchester into the bar knocking bodies flying in all directions and receiving fire back, but luckily mainly small calibre and not automatic.

That was soon to change as the front door of the pub flew open and my old friend Laurie still with his nose spread all over his face from where I'd smacked him with the butt of my gun last summer, got into the act with a twin to the Heckler & Koch MP5 that was still slung over my shoulder.

74

HE OPENED FIRE and I threw myself behind the bar next to Brenda as his fusillade of nine millimetre slugs chewed up the carpet and the wood of the counter sending splinters flying like killer bees. I unhitched my H&K and pushed it around the side of the bar and fired it one handed so that it jumped and juddered in my fist and Laurie hit the deck.

But then it all started to go pear shaped; as Brenda rose to fire her Uzi, and I went to change the clip on the H&K, two of the doors on the mezzanine above us flew open and a pair of armed men came crashing through and fired down between the bannisters spinning Brenda round and opening a wound in her shoulder. She dropped the gun, and I looked up to see twin barrels pointed straight at me.

'Drop it,' ordered one of the men.

I thought about going for the Glock in its shoulder holster but I saw the determination in his eyes and did as I was told.

'That's better,' he said. 'Now stand up, both of you.'

I helped Brenda to her feet. Her face was ashen and she was losing a lot of blood. 'She needs attention,' I said.

'Forget it,' said Laurie as he picked himself up from where he was lying by the door. 'I'll give her all the attention she needs.'

'At least let me stop the bleeding,' I pleaded. 'She'll die.'

'We're all going to die,' cut in a reedy voice and Marco appeared on the mezzanine too. 'Just some of us will take longer than others. Go on then. But no tricks. One false move and you'll both die very quickly.'

I picked up a tattered dish cloth from on top of the bar, folded it four times, pulled off Brenda's jacket, winced at all the blood, found the wound, covered it with the cloth and put her hand on top. 'Keep up a firm pressure,' I said 'You'll be fine.'

'Sorry John,' she said.

'Don't mention it,' I replied. 'You did good. Very good.'

Marco strutted down the stairs with his two sidekicks and

came towards us. Laurie fell in behind. 'Search them,' the little man ordered. 'And don't forget he keeps a gun in his boot.'

Laurie did as he was told and got all our guns, including my .38, but missed the grenade round my neck just like I'd hoped he would. These boys were crap and I intended to show them just how bad they were before I was finished at The Last Chance Saloon.

75

'**SO WE MEET AGAIN**,' said Marco. 'I'm sorry that you were away when we called at your little farm.'

'You were lucky I was.'

'No. You were lucky. Or you would've ended up with your girl friend.' He gestured with his thumb in the direction of Loretta's head that stared sightlessly down on us from the stake where it had been impaled, and I felt such a rush of anger that I thought that my brain would burst. But I had to stay calm. I looked at my watch. Just a few minutes to go and I needed to stay alive through every one of them. 'But it's not too late,' he continued. 'You and this woman will make up the set. You were bloody fools to come here.'

'Don't you believe it,' I replied with a voice I could hear shook with emotion, but from Marco's smug smile I knew he took it to be fear. 'You were bloody fools to leave her alive. Because she saved the most important person there.'

'What do you mean?' he demanded.

'Loretta's baby.'

'What?'

'You didn't know that she was pregnant when I took her away did you? Well she was. And the baby lived. It was close. He was ill for a while, but he got better. He was immune. The first of a new generation post The Death. So there's hope for the human race after all. No thanks to scum like you and your cronies here. And I'm telling you now little man, if I didn't intend to destroy this evil place, to flatten it, to raze it to the ground, to erase it as if it had never existed, I'd make sure your head was up there with hers. Except that would be an insult to her memory.'

He laughed out loud at that. 'Now I'm really terrified,' he said and turned to Laurie 'Kill them,' he ordered. 'But make it last.'

I checked my watch. There was barely a minute to go before the detonator was due to blow and I looked at Laurie and grinned. 'The nose suits you,' I said. 'Gives your face character.'

'I'm going to enjoy this,' he said, but it was too late. I glanced at my watch again and then as the sweep hand hit the twelve the Range Rover parked outside exploded, the generator building blew with it, the generator itself self-destructed, and all the lights in the building went out.

76

IF THERE WAS CHAOS in the room before, after the explosion it was even worse. In the light of the flickering flames from the burning outhouse that intermittently lit the room I reached out for Brenda's hand and pulled her in the direction of the bar counter where our weapons had been piled. Someone opened fire with an automatic weapon as we went, someone else screamed as they were hit, and I grabbed the H&K I'd been loading and pulled the trigger spewing out thirty bullets in less time than it takes to tell.

More screams of agony. More yelling of conflicting orders. Brenda picked up my loaded Glock in one hand and her Colt in the other and began methodically firing into the packed bodies despite her injury.

The place was like an abattoir. There were bodies everywhere, lying where they'd fallen in all sorts of grotesque positions. It was like a scene from some Hieronymus Bosch painting in the flickering light from outside.

And there in front of me, screaming the loudest of all was little Marco. His empire was crumbling, and despite myself I was laughing. Laughing fit to bust. Laughing like I hadn't laughed for a year or more. Since The Death came and took my family and made me what I was now.

And, he could see and hear me laughing and I think that scared him so much he didn't even take his opportunity to finish me.

So I finished him.

I reached inside my shirt and felt the reassuring weight of the grenade in my hand. It fitted like it had been made for me and me alone, and I tugged it off its lanyard and the pin flew across the room. And with my other hand I tugged his tunic open and stuffed the grenade inside and pushed him back so that he stumbled and fell, and I threw myself back behind the safety of the bar as the grenade exploded and all sorts of nasty stuff flew around the room. The sound of the explosion temporarily deafened me and my voice sounded strange as I screamed for Brenda but she was gone. A bullet, or shrapnel from the grenade had torn open her stomach and she lay next to me, her life ebbing away and although I tried to help it was too late.

I ignored everything else in trying to help her, and if some chancer had looked over the top of the counter he could've finished me in a second. But that wasn't my destiny. In fact, when I stood up a few minutes later the inside of the Last Chance Saloon was empty except for the dead and dying.

The grenade had started several small fires and I added to them by tossing a bottle of whisky onto the floor where it broke and spread the flames.

It seemed to me I was getting good at setting fires and I wasn't finished yet.

I found my Glock, reloaded it and put it in its holster. The other weapons I left where they lay.

Puppy was lying by the door her paws over her ears and I called her in that strange voice I heard echoing in my ears and when I checked her for injuries there wasn't a mark on her.

We went out into the night together and the snow had stopped and all that was left in the car park was the wrecks of the cars and bikes that had been destroyed in the explosion. There wasn't a human being to be seen.

'Seems like we're all alone Pup,' I said as the flames licked at the inside of the building. 'Just one more thing to do. Stay here.'

I walked through the wreckage of the fence around the compound to where the three tankers were parked. They were on a slight incline, parallel to each other and I turned the stopcock on the tank of the one at the top of the slope until petrol began to pour out and splash my shoes.

I watched as the fuel hit the ground and began to run downhill melting the snow as it went. The liquid ran beneath the second tanker, then the third and inexorably down towards the helicopter until it reached its undercarriage and began to puddle there. The air stunk of petrol and even in that temperature the fumes hung above the gush and teared my eyes.

I walked back to where Puppy was patiently waiting and

fished around for my last cigarette. I put it in my mouth, lit it with my Zippo lighter, took a drag and let out the smoke and my breath into the freezing air like a cloud.

'I reckon I'll be giving these up again now,' I said, took the cigarette, fitted it between my forefinger and thumb and flicked it into the air, and watched as coal of the cigarette forged a red arc through the air and into the petrol.

Just before it landed I screamed, 'Run girl,' and we took off towards the gatehouse.

The explosion knocked us both flat into a snowdrift, and I turned, wiped the wet out of my eyes and watched the tankers and the chopper blow themselves into the sort of firework display I hadn't witnessed since Millennium night. The ammunition stored at the back of the building exploded, sending strings of tracer into the sky like diamond necklaces of cold fire.

WE LAY THERE, my dog and me, until the pyrotechnics had finished, the smoke was cloaking the stars and Marco's empire had been destroyed like it had never existed. As if a squadron of Phantom jets had napalmed the shit out of the place.

Then, wearily, we climbed out of the snow drift, I brushed the wet off myself as well as I could, Puppy shook freezing drops of water off her coat and we walked away from The Last Chance Saloon without looking back.

We needed somewhere warm and dry to spend the night, food to eat and water to drink, before we could get on with our lives. Somewhere up the road it was waiting I knew. If we could get through the last few days, a place to sleep was the least of our worries.

And it was there like I knew it would be, and it led somewhere else and somewhere else again.

So what did happen after?

Well, Puppy and I saw things we never knew existed in our wildest dreams, but that's a whole other story.